Enid Blyton
CHRISTMAS TREATS

Look out for all of these enchanting story collections by

Enid Blyton

CHRISTMAS COLLECTIONS
Christmas Stories
Christmas Tales
Christmas Treats

SUMMER COLLECTIONS
Holiday Stories
Summer Holiday Stories
Summer Stories

OTHER COLLECTIONS
Brer Rabbit
Cherry Tree Farm
Fireworks in Fairyland
Mr Galliano's Circus
Stories of Wizards and Witches
The Wizard's Umbrella

Enid Blyton

CHRISTMAS TREATS

*Hodder
Children's
Books*

HODDER CHILDREN'S BOOKS

This collection first published in Great Britain in 2017 by
Hodder and Stoughton

1 3 5 7 9 10 8 6 4 2

Enid Blyton ®
Enid Blyton's signature is a Registered Trademark of
Hodder and Stoughton Limited
Text copyright © Hodder and Stoughton Limited, 2017
Illustrations by Mark Beech, © Hodder and Stoughton Limited, 2017

A CIP catalogue record for this book is available from the British Library.

ISBN 978 1 444 93668 1

Typeset in Caslon Twelve by Avon DataSet Ltd,
Bidford-on-Avon, Warwickshire

Printed and bound in Great Britain by Clays Ltd, St Ives plc

The paper and board used in this book are made from wood
from responsible sources

MIX
Paper from
responsible sources
FSC® C104740

Hodder Children's Books
An imprint of
Hachette Children's Group
Part of Hodder and Stoughton
Carmelite House
50 Victoria Embankment
London EC4Y 0DZ

An Hachette UK Company
www.hachette.co.uk
www.hachettechildrens.co.uk

Contents

Santa's Workshop   1

Christmas at Last!   19

The Christmas Pudding that Wouldn't Stop   33

The Wishing Glove   55

Mr Icy-Cold   71

The Fairies' Christmas Party   83

The Christmas Party   95

Pins and Needles!   101

Mr Loud-Voice Makes a Mistake   107

What's Happened to Michael?   117

Mr Widdle's Christmas Stocking   133

Who Could It Be?   139

The Battle in the Toyshop   149

Surprise on Christmas Morning   159

Rescuing Santa Claus   171

The Astonishing Christmas Tree   185

A Christmas Story   197

Do-As-You're-Told!   203

Something in His Stocking   213

Mr Pink-Whistle and Santa Claus   225

On Christmas Night   241

The Great Big Snowman   247

Peter's Christmas Surprise   257

Bunny's First Christmas   263

The Best Christmas Tree of All   277

Wanted – A Royal Snow-Digger   285

The Pantomime Cat   295

The Three Strange Travellers   305

Mr Twiddle and the Snow   325

Acknowledgements   337

Santa's Workshop

Santa's Workshop

IN THE nursery all the toys were getting ready for Christmas. The dolls' house dolls were making paper chains and the wind-up sailor was baking mince pies. Even Panda was helping to make decorations, and he had only arrived in the nursery three weeks before – a present from the children's Aunt Jane.

All the toys were helping, except for one – the big rocking horse that lived in the middle of the nursery floor. He was a fine fellow with a lovely spotted coat, a big mane and a bushy black tail.

He rocked back and forth and took the children for long rides around the nursery floor. They all loved him – but the toys were afraid of him.

Sometimes he would begin to rock when they were playing around, and then, how they ran out of the way!

Sometimes he was so proud and so vain that he would not play with the other nursery toys.

'I'm too important to do boring things like making paper chains,' he boasted. 'I'm the only toy in this nursery big enough for the children to ride on. I ought to be king of the nursery for Christmas.'

'Well, you don't deserve to be,' said the curly-haired doll. 'You squashed the monkey's tail yesterday, and that was unkind.'

'I didn't mean to,' said the horse, offended. 'He shouldn't have left it lying around under my rockers. Silly of him.'

'You should have looked down before you began to rock, and you would have seen it,' said the doll.

'Well! Do you suppose I'm going to bother to look for tails and things before I begin to rock?' said the horse. 'You just look out for yourselves! That's the best thing to do.'

But the toys were careless. Later that morning the little red toy car ran under the horse's rockers and had his paint badly scratched. Next, the wind-up sailor left his key there and the rocking horse bent it when he rocked on it. It was difficult to wind up the sailor after that, and he was cross.

Then the curly-haired doll dropped her bead necklace and the rocking horse rocked on it and smashed some of the beads. The toys were really upset with him about that.

'Be careful, be careful!' they cried. 'Tell us before you rock, Rocking horse! You might rock on one of us and hurt us badly!'

But the rocking horse just laughed and thought it was a great joke to scare the toys so much.

'You are not kind,' said Ben the big teddy bear. 'One day you will be sorry.'

And so he was, as you will hear.

It happened that, on the day before Christmas, Sarah and Jack had been playing with their toys and had left them all around the nursery when they had gone for lunch.

Now, the panda's head and one of his ears were just under the rocker of the rocking horse. And as soon as the children had left the room the rocking horse decided to rock.

'Stop! Stop!' shrieked the toys, running forward. 'Panda is underneath!'

But the rocking horse didn't listen. No, he thought the toys were scared as usual, and he didn't listen to what they said. Back and forth he rocked – and poor Panda was underneath!

Oh dear, oh dear, when the toys got to him what a sight he was! Some of his nice black fur had come out, and his right ear was all squashed. The toys pulled him away and began to cry.

'What's the matter?' asked the rocking horse, stopping and looking down.

'You naughty horse! We told you to stop! Now see what you have done!' cried the toys angrily. 'You are really very unkind. We won't speak to you or play with you any more.'

'Don't then,' said the horse, and he rocked away by himself. *Cree-eek, cree-eek!* 'I'm sure I don't want to talk to you or give you rides if you are going to be so cross with me.'

After that the toys paid no attention to the naughty rocking horse.

They made a great fuss over Panda, who soon stopped crying. Then they went on getting ready for Christmas. Ben wrapped up a present for the pink cat, Rag Doll made a Christmas stocking, and Jack-in-the-box helped the other toys hang tinsel on the Christmas tree. They had such fun!

In the corner of the nursery, Rocking horse felt sad. He usually helped hang the tinsel because he could reach higher than the other toys.

I wish they'd talk to me! he thought to himself.

7

I wish they'd play. I'd like to give them each a ride around the nursery – in fact, I'd take three of them at once if they asked me.

But the toys acted as if the rocking horse wasn't there at all. They didn't ask him to help with anything. They didn't even look at him.

'He's unkind and selfish and horrid,' they said. 'And the best way to treat people like that is not to pay any attention to them.'

So the rocking horse got sadder and sadder, and longed to gallop around the nursery just for a change. But he was afraid the toys might be cross if he did.

Now, just as it was getting dark the children's puppy came into the nursery, because someone had left the door open. The toys fled to the toy cupboard in fear, because the puppy was very playful and liked to carry a toy outdoors and chew it.

Everyone got safely into the cupboard except the pink cat. She slipped and fell, and the puppy pounced on her. He chewed and nibbled her whiskers clean away! Nobody dared to rescue her, not even the rocking horse, though he did wonder if he should gallop at the puppy.

Then somebody whistled from downstairs, and the puppy flew out of the door.

The poor pink cat sat up.

'Oh!' she said. 'Whatever has happened to my fine pink whiskers?'

'They've gone,' said Panda, peeping out of the cupboard. 'The puppy has chewed them off. There they are, look, on the floor, in tiny little bits.'

The pink cat cried bitterly. She had been proud of her whiskers. 'A cat doesn't look like a cat without her whiskers,' she wept.

The sound of the pink cat crying made Panda feel so sad that soon he was crying too.

'What shall we do?' he wailed. 'Oh, what shall we do? When Sarah and Jack see us, all nibbled and squashed, they will throw us into the dustbin. Boo-hoo-hoo!'

'Yes,' sobbed the pink cat. 'They won't want us if they are given brand-new toys for Christmas.' And before long the nursery was filled with the sound of toys crying.

How the rocking horse wished he had not been so unkind! He would miss any of the toys terribly if they were thrown away – and it would be mostly his fault, too! Whatever could he do to earn their forgiveness? He looked around the nursery at all the Christmas decorations and suddenly he knew just what to do.

'Excuse me, toys – but I've got an idea,' he said in his humblest voice.

'It's only the rocking horse,' said Ben. 'Don't pay any attention to him.'

'Please do pay some attention,' said the horse. 'I've got a good idea. I can take all the broken toys to Santa Claus's workshop. I know the way because I came from there. Perhaps Santa Claus can fix you all and make you better.'

'But it's Christmas Eve!' cried Panda. 'Santa will be too busy delivering presents to have time for *us*.'

'Oh no!' replied Rocking horse. 'Santa is the friend of every old toy. No matter how busy he is, I'm sure he will find time to help us if we ask him tonight!'

'Well! Let's go then,' said the teddy bear. So the toys helped Pink Cat and Panda, Wind-up Sailor and the monkey, Curly-haired Doll and the little red toy car all up on to Rocking horse's back. Then Ben sat at the very front and said,

'Let's go!'

Cree-eek, cree-eek! went Rocking horse, across the nursery floor and up, away out of the window and into the night sky. For miles and miles they travelled, rocking past twinkling stars towards the great hill where Santa Claus lived.

Luckily for the toys, Santa was at home. He was busy piling a new load of presents on to his magic sleigh. His faithful reindeer would take them fast and far – to the other side of the world in the blink of an eye. When he heard the sound of the rocking horse neighing and hrrumphing at the door, he came to see who was there.

Rocking horse explained why they had come and, to the toys' delight, Santa said he would be glad to help. He only had three more loads to deliver before morning. Then he inspected each of the toys in turn to see what the damage was.

'Dear, dear!' said Santa Claus, looking severely at the rocking horse. 'I hope you are ashamed of yourself. I have heard of you and your stupid ways of scaring the toys by rocking suddenly when they are near. Come in!'

The horse rocked in and followed Santa Claus to his workshop. In no time at all Santa had straightened out Wind-up Sailor's key and mended the curly-haired doll's broken beads. He soon fixed the monkey's squashed tail and patched up the toy car's scratched paint.

Then it was Panda's turn. Santa opened a

drawer and looked into it.

'Dear me!' he said. 'I've no panda fur left. It's all been used up. Now what am I to do?'

He turned and looked at the rocking horse.

'You've a nice thick black mane!' he said. 'I think you'll have to spare a little for Panda!'

Then, to the rocking horse's horror, he took out a pair of scissors and cut a patch out of his thick mane! How strange it looked!

Quickly and neatly, Santa Claus put the black fur on to the panda's head. He stuck it there with glue, and it soon dried. Then Santa looked at Panda's squashed ear.

He found a new ear and carefully put it on. It belonged to a teddy bear, really, so it was brown, instead of black, and looked rather odd.

'Now I've no special black paint!' said Santa in a vexed tone. 'Only blue or red. That won't do for a panda's ear. Ha, I'll have to take off one of your nice black spots, Rocking horse, and use it for the panda's ear. That will do nicely!'

He carefully scraped off a large spot on the horse's back, mixed it with a tiny drop of water and then painted it on Panda's new ear. It looked fine!

'Thank you very much indeed!' said the panda, gratefully. 'You are very kind.'

'Not at all!' said Santa, beaming all over his big, kind face. 'I'm always ready to help toys, you know! And how can I help you?' he said, looking at the pink cat. She soon explained all about her whiskers.

'Oh dear, oh dear, oh dear!' said Santa shaking his head sadly. 'I'm right out of whiskers.'

Just then, a small voice piped up behind him. It was Rocking horse.

'I should be very pleased to give the toy cat some of the hairs out of my long black tail,' he said. 'They would do beautifully for whiskers.'

'But how can we get them out?' said the pink cat.

'Pull them out, of course,' said the horse.

'But it will hurt you,' said the pink cat.

14

'I don't mind,' said the horse, bravely. 'Pull as many as you like!' So Santa pulled eight out, and they did hurt. But the horse didn't make a sound.

Then Santa carefully gave the cat her whiskers back.

'One whisker!' he said. 'Two whiskers! Three whiskers! Oh, you will look fine when I have finished, Pink Cat. These are black whiskers, long and strong, and you will look very handsome now.' And so she did. Very fine indeed!

At last it was time to go, so all the toys clambered back on to the rocking horse.

'Thank you Santa,' they cried as they left. 'Thank you for helping us all.'

Then off they went home again, rocking hard all the way in order to get home by morning, and glad to be good as new again.

The toys cheered when they saw them.

'What glorious fur you have – and look at your fine new ear!' they cried when they saw Panda. 'And look at your lovely whiskers,' they said to Pink Cat.

Rocking horse said nothing. He stood in the middle of the nursery floor, quite still, not a rock left in him.

'Santa took some of Rocking horse's hair for me, and one of his spots to paint my ear black,' said Panda. 'You can see where he has a bare place on his mane, and one of his biggest spots is missing.'

Sure enough, it was just as Panda had said.

'I must say it was nice of the rocking horse to give you them,' said Ben, suddenly.

'And to give me my new whiskers,' added Pink Cat. 'Especially as we haven't even spoken to him lately. Very nice of him.'

All the other toys thought the same. So, they went over to the rocking horse who was still looking sad.

'Thank you for taking us to Santa's workshop,' said the curly-haired doll.

'It was very kind of you,' said the monkey.

'I can't thank you enough!' said the pink cat. 'I had

pink whiskers before, and they didn't show up very well – but these show beautifully. Don't you think so?'

'You look very handsome,' said the horse. 'Very!'

'Your tail looks a bit thin now, I'm afraid,' said the pink cat. 'Do you mind?'

'Not a bit,' said the rocking horse. 'I can rock back and forth just as fast when my tail is thin as when it's thick. You get on my back and see, Pink Cat!'

So up got the pink cat, and the rocking horse went rocking around the nursery at top speed. It was very exciting. You may be sure the horse looked where he was going this time! He wasn't going to rock over anyone's tail again!

'Oh, thank you!' said the pink cat, quite out of breath. 'That was the nicest ride I ever had!'

'Anyone can have one!' said the horse, rather gruffly, because he was afraid that the toys might say 'No,' and turn their backs on him.

But they didn't. They all climbed up at once.

'Nice old horse!' they said. 'We're friends again now, aren't we? Gallop away, gallop away!'

And you should have seen him gallop away again, around and around the nursery until the sun peeped through the curtains.

'Merry Christmas, Merry Christmas,' they heard the children shouting.

'Good gracious,' said Ben the teddy bear. 'It's Christmas Day!' All the toys had quite forgotten.

And a lovely Christmas Day it turned out to be, too. Sarah and Jack were amazed at how smart all their old toys looked – apart from Rocking horse, whose mane and tail looked a bit straggly.

'Never mind,' said Sarah. 'We will always love you, toys, even if you are old and worn, won't we Jack?'

'Oh yes,' said Jack. 'Merry Christmas toys. Merry Christmas to you all!'

Christmas at Last!

Christmas at Last!

'CHRISTMAS IS coming,' said Bobs to Bimbo and Topsy. Bobs was a black-and-white fox terrier.

'Who's he?' asked Topsy, the fox terrier puppy. 'A visitor?'

'No, silly,' said Bobs. 'Christmas is a day – we all get presents and everyone is happy.'

'Who brings the presents?' asked Bimbo.

'Santa Claus, of course,' said Bobs.

'Any relation of mine?' asked Bimbo, the naughty Siamese kitten, stretching out his twenty claws for everyone to see. 'I'm Bimbo Claws, as you can see. Is Santa Claus an uncle of mine, do you think?'

'Don't be funny,' said Bobs. 'Santa Claus is a kind old gentleman. Gillian and Imogen call up the chimney to tell him what they want in their Christmas stockings. They hang up a stocking each, and Santa Claus fills it on Christmas Eve. We had better hang up stockings too. It would be lovely to find bones and chews and biscuits in them, wouldn't it!'

'That seems a very good idea,' said Bimbo, sitting up. 'Did you say this nice old gentleman lives up the chimney?'

'No, I didn't,' said Bobs. 'I said that the children call up the chimney to tell him what they want.'

'Well, if he can hear them, he must be up the chimney then,' said Topsy. 'Bimbo, you're used to chimneys. You climb up them all, one by one, and see which one Santa Claus lives in.'

'No thank you,' said Bimbo. 'No more chimneys for me. We'll call up, though, and say what we want, shall we?'

'And we'll hang up stockings too,' said Cosy, the tabby cat.

'We haven't got any,' said Topsy. 'We don't wear them. Can't we hang up our collars instead?'

'I suppose you think our collars would easily hold things like biscuits and chews,' said Bobs. 'I do think you are silly sometimes, Topsy.'

'Well, you be clever and tell us what to do about stockings then,' said Topsy, snapping at Bobs's tail.

'Don't do that,' said Bobs. 'Let me think a minute. Oh, I know!'

'What?' cried Topsy, Bimbo and Cosy.

'Well, you know that the children's socks are hung up on the line to dry, don't you?' said Bobs. 'Well, what about jumping up and getting some for ourselves? We can easily do that!'

So the next day all four of them went to look at the clothes line. And, sure enough, there were two pairs of long socks there, one belonging to Imogen and one to Gillian. It wasn't long before Bobs was jumping up to get hold of one.

But he couldn't get high enough. So Cosy tried. She caught hold of a sock with her claws. She hung on for all she was worth and, oh dear, the clothes line broke, and all the clothes fell in a heap on poor Cosy!

How scared she was! She tore off down the garden with the line wound round her body, and all the clothes galloped after her!

It was the funniest sight to see. Bobs, Topsy and Bimbo sat down and laughed till they cried. But when their mistress came out and saw how all the clean clothes had been dragged in the mud, she wasn't a bit pleased. Cosy got a scolding and sat and sulked all by herself in the corner.

'That was a very bad idea of yours,' she said to Bobs.

But when Christmas Eve came, what a lovely surprise! Gillian and Imogen came into the playroom with four stockings and showed them to the surprised animals.

'You shall hang up your stockings just as we do!' said Imogen. 'Here is one for you, Bobs, and one for you, Topsy, and smaller ones for the cats.'

The four stockings were hung just above the animals' baskets. They did look funny, hanging limp and thin and empty.

'If you go to sleep, and don't peep, perhaps Santa Claus will come down the chimney here in the night and fill these stockings for you,' said Imogen. 'Perhaps you will have a new collar, Bobs – and you a rubber bone, Topsy – and you a ball to roll about, Bimbo – and you a new rug for your basket, Cosy. And maybe you will have biscuits and sardines and bones and other nice things as well! So go to sleep and don't make a sound, in case you frighten Santa Claus away!'

'Isn't this exciting?' said Topsy, when the children had gone out of the room. 'I'm going to settle down in my basket and go to sleep straight away!'

'So am I,' said Bimbo. 'Ooh, I do hope I shall get a

tin of sardines. I wonder if Santa Claus will have any in his sack?'

'I really would love a new collar,' said Bobs. 'Mine is so old. Well – good night to you all. I'm going to sleep too. And if we hear old Father Christmas, we mustn't peep! Do you hear, Topsy? No peeping!'

'Well, don't you peep either,' said Topsy. 'And don't think he is a robber or something when he comes, and bark at him, or you'll frighten him away! Good night, everyone!'

And very soon all the animals were fast asleep. Bobs and Cosy were curled up together in one big basket, and Bimbo and Topsy were fast asleep in the small one.

They dreamt that their stockings were full of all the things that animals love: bones and biscuits, sardines and kippers, balls and saucers of cream!

In the morning the four animals awoke. Topsy woke first and put her head out of the basket. She sniffed hard. She could smell a lovely smell.

'Oh! It's Christmas morning!' she wuffed in Bimbo's ear. Bimbo woke up with a jump.

'What about our stockings?' he said. 'Did Santa Claus come in the night and fill them? I didn't hear him.'

'Look!' cried Bobs, waking up too. 'Our stockings are crammed full! I can smell bones.'

'And I can smell sardines!' cried Cosy. All the animals got out of their baskets and sniffed round the exciting stockings.

'A new collar for me!' barked Bobs, dragging one out in delight. 'Just look at it; brass studs all the way round. My goodness, I shall look grand. I wish I had a tie to go with it, like men wear.'

'A rubber bone for me!' wuffed Topsy, and she took the bone from her stocking and tried to chew it. But the more she chewed at the bone, the less she seemed to eat of it. Most peculiar!

'That bone will last you for years,' said Bobs with a

grin. 'It's all chew and no taste! Give me a real bone any day!'

'A fine new ball for me!' mewed Bimbo, rolling a lovely red ball over the floor. 'Come and play with me, Topsy. Throw it into the air and make it bounce.'

'What about my new rug?' said Cosy, dragging a knitted rug into her basket and lying down on it. 'Now this is what I call a really nice present. I shall be able to lie on it and keep myself warm, and you, Bobs, will be able to hide all kinds of goodies under it, to keep till you want them.'

'What, hide them under your rug for you to nibble at when I'm not there!' cried Bobs. 'No, thank you, Cosy. Oh, tails and whiskers, there are other things in our stockings too! A real big bone for me, full of crunch and nibble!'

'And there's a tin of sardines for me and Bimbo,' said Cosy. 'Oh, I hope Gillian and Imogen come along quickly to open it. I just feel as if I could do with three or four sardines inside me.'

'There are biscuits at the bottom of *my* stocking,' said Topsy, putting her head right down to the bottom of the stocking and nosing about in the toe. 'Biscuits! Big ones and little ones! I'll give you each one if you like.'

She got some in her mouth, but, dear me, when she wanted to take out her head and give the biscuits to the others, she couldn't get rid of the stocking. It stuck fast over her head and Topsy ran about the room in the stocking. The others did laugh!

Then in came Gillian and Imogen. 'Happy Christmas, Bobs, Topsy, Bimbo and Cosy!' they cried. 'Oh, Topsy, whatever are you doing? What are you wearing that stocking on your head for? Did you think it was a hat?'

They pulled the stocking from Topsy's head, and the four animals crowded round the children. Topsy was glad to have her head out of the stocking.

'Here's a bar of chocolate for you two girls,' said Bobs, and he pulled one out from his basket. 'I've sat on it for the last week, I'm afraid, so it's a bit squashy, but the taste is still there, because I've tried it each morning.'

'And here's one of my very best biscuits,' said Topsy, fetching one from her basket. 'It's the biggest one I have had in my dinner bowl for weeks. Try it. I've nibbled a pattern all round the edge to make it pretty for you.'

'And I've been into the hen run and collected you a few feathers,' said Cosy. 'I hope they'll be useful. Good gracious, Bimbo – whatever have you got there?'

'My collection of kipper heads from the rubbish heaps all round,' said Bimbo proudly. 'They're the best I could find. I hid them in the landing cupboard in a hatbox there.'

'Gracious! That was what made that awful smell, I suppose!' said Gillian. 'And, oh dear, Bimbo, Mummy keeps one of her best hats in that box. I can't imagine what she'll say if she goes out smelling of kippers.'

'I should think she'll be very pleased,' said Bimbo.

'Kippers have a gorgeous smell. I'm surprised people don't make scent of them, instead of silly things like honeysuckle and sweetpeas!'

'Well, thank you all very much,' said Gillian. 'You've given us lovely presents. Now let's all go to breakfast, and we'll show you the presents we had too!'

So off they all went, Bobs wearing his new collar, and Topsy carrying her rubber bone for another long chew. Cosy had to leave her rug behind, but Bimbo rolled his ball all the way to the dining room.

The sardines were opened, and Cosy and Bimbo shared them with the dogs.

'Delicious,' they all said, and licked their whiskers clean.

They had a lovely Christmas, and even had a taste of the great big turkey. They had a special supper that evening of biscuits soaked in turkey gravy, and then, full of good things, they all went to their baskets to sleep.

CHRISTMAS TREATS

They curled up together, put their noses between their paws, and dreamt lovely dreams of sardines, bones, collars and balls! And there we will leave them, dreaming happily.

The
Christmas Pudding
that Wouldn't Stop

The Christmas Pudding that Wouldn't Stop

GUBBLEUP AND GUBBLEDOWN were two little goblins and they lived in Gubble Cottage. They were both dressed exactly the same in little high caps, green tunics and green leggings, but you could never mistake one for the other, for Gubbleup was very tall and thin, and Gubbledown was very small and fat.

It was nearly Christmas time, and Gubbleup and Gubbledown had been to a great many parties.

'We really ought to give a party ourselves,' said Gubbleup.

'Yes, we ought,' said Gubbledown. 'We've been to so many. What about having one tomorrow?'

'Have you got any money?' asked Gubbleup.

Gubbledown turned out his pockets.

'I've got two pennies and a halfpenny,' he said. 'That wouldn't go far towards paying for a party. How much have you got, Gubbleup?'

Gubbleup took down a little china pig from the mantelpiece and unscrewed its head. Inside were some pennies, halfpennies and a silver threepenny bit.

'One threepenny bit, three pennies and three halfpennies,' he said.

'What does your money and mine make altogether?' asked Gubbledown.

'That's very difficult,' sighed Gubbleup, taking a pencil from his pocket. 'It's the sort of sum we did when we were at school. Now let me see – one threepenny bit, three pennies, three halfpennies, two pennies of yours and a halfpenny.'

After a great deal of thinking and scribbling and rubbing-out, the goblins decided that they had exactly two shillings.

'Oh dear – that won't go far towards buying things to eat,' sighed Gubbleup.

'We must have a Christmas pudding,' said Gubbledown, firmly. 'You can't have a Christmas party without a Christmas pudding.'

'But how can we have a Christmas pudding?' asked Gubbleup. 'They cost a lot of money – and besides, we don't know how to make one.'

'Well, let's go and ask the old Sugarstick Gnome if he'll make us one for a shilling,' said Gubbledown. 'If he will, we can spend the other shilling on jellies and cakes, and that will be enough for a party.'

'The Sugarstick Gnome won't make one for a shilling!' said Gubbleup. 'Don't be silly!'

'I'm not silly,' said Gubbledown, offended. 'Come on, and we'll see.'

So the two goblins put on their pointed caps, and went through the wood to the Sugarstick Gnome's.

He lived in a funny shop, whose chimneys

looked like barley sugar sticks, and whose walls were as brown as chocolate. His pretty curtains had a pattern of cakes, tarts and sweets all over them, and altogether his shop was a most exciting one to visit.

The Sugarstick Gnome made puddings and pies, cakes and tarts, sweets and chocolate. He had a little kitchen at the back of the shop, and here he made everything. No one knew how he made his goods, for he always kept his kitchen door shut and the curtains drawn tightly across the window.

There was never any smell of cooking at the shop of the Sugarstick Gnome. So people said that he made all his goodies by magic – but nobody knew exactly how.

Gubbleup and Gubbledown soon reached the shop, opened the door, and went in.

No one was there.

The two goblins waited for some minutes, and then grew impatient.

'Wherever can the Sugarstick Gnome be?' exclaimed Gubbleup.

Gubbledown rapped on the counter.

Nobody came.

The kitchen door was shut, and no sound came from the kitchen.

'Perhaps the Sugarstick Gnome is ill,' said Gubbleup at last.

'Shall we go into the kitchen and see?' asked Gubbledown.

'No,' said Gubbleup. 'He might be cross. People say he has a very bad temper. We don't want to be turned into peppermint lumps or anything.'

'Good gracious!' said Gubbledown, startled. 'I should think not. But what can we do, Gubbleup? I'm getting tired of waiting here. And he may be ill, you know.'

'Well, let's go and see if we can peep into the kitchen window,' said Gubbleup, jumping off his chair.

So the two goblins ran out of the shop and went

round the garden to the back window. The curtains were drawn tightly over the window – all but a little crack at one side.

'We could peep in through this crack!' whispered Gubbledown, and put his eye to it.

What he saw made him stare in astonishment.

The Sugarstick Gnome was not ill. He was making Christmas puddings. There they were, spread out in delicious rows on the table.

But dear me, he made them in a most extraordinary way!

The goblins saw him take up a tiny black currant and put it on a plate. Then he danced solemnly round it, and chanted an odd song:

'Little black currant of mine
Make me a pudding, I pray,
A Christmas pudding as fine
As anyone's baking today!'

Then right before Gubbleup's and Gubbledown's astonished eyes the currant seemed to swell, and gradually a fine plum pudding grew up on the plate. It grew bigger and bigger and bigger, until it was as large as a pumpkin.

The two goblins were so surprised that they sat down on the grass outside and stared at each other.

'So that's how he makes all his things!' whispered Gubbledown. 'What powerful magic must be in that currant!'

'Let's peep again!' said Gubbleup. Once more the goblins put their eyes to the crack and looked.

The Sugarstick Gnome was just taking out the magic currant to use again for another pudding. Immediately the first pudding stopped growing.

The goblins watched him put the currant on an empty plate, and heard him sing the magic song again. Once more a pudding grew.

Gubbleup and Gubbledown didn't wait for the end of that one. They marched back into the shop, and stamped loudly on the floor.

'If he's got so many, surely he can sell us one cheaply,' said Gubbledown, hoisting his fat little body up on a chair.

The Sugarstick Gnome came into the shop, and shut his kitchen door behind him.

'Good morning,' said Gubbleup. 'Would you please sell us a big Christmas pudding for a shilling?'

The Sugarstick Gnome laughed.

'No, I won't,' he said. 'Big puddings cost four shillings.'

'Oh dear,' said the goblins in dismay. 'Are you sure you couldn't?'

'Quite,' said the Sugarstick Gnome. 'Anything else you'd like?'

Gubbleup and Gubbledown were most disappointed.

'Oh well,' said Gubbleup, sighing. 'I suppose we'd better make do with cakes and jelly. How many can you let us have for two shillings?'

'One red jelly, two yellow jellies, six chocolate cakes, six cream buns, and twelve currant cakes,' said the Sugarstick Gnome. 'Very cheap, too.'

'All right,' said Gubbleup. 'We'll call for them tomorrow at two o'clock. We're going to have a party in the afternoon, so please have them ready.'

The goblins paid over their money and went out. They were so disappointed about the pudding that for a minute or two neither of them spoke a word.

Gubbledown heaved a sigh.

'It won't be much of a Christmas party without a Christmas pudding,' he sighed.

'No,' said Gubbleup. 'Still, we shall have twenty-four cakes and three jellies, and you know we've got a tin of chocolate biscuits.'

'And we'll make some lemonade,' said Gubbledown, cheering up. 'And play lots of jolly games.'

'Let's call and ask everybody now,' said Gubbleup.

So the goblins called on their friends, and asked

them all to come to their party the next day. Everyone was most delighted and accepted at once.

Then the two goblins hurried home and cleaned up their living room. They put holly all round the pictures, and made paper chains to go across the ceiling. That took them all the day, and they went to bed tired out.

Next morning they were most excited. Gubbleup made the lemonade, and Gubbledown got out the tin of chocolate biscuits and arranged them in nice little patterns on blue plates.

Then he got out all his best glasses and washed them ready for the party.

By that time it was a quarter to two, and the goblins thought they had better fetch the jellies and cakes from the Sugarstick Gnome's.

'Everybody's coming at three o'clock,' said Gubbleup putting on his cap. 'So we'd better hurry, Gubbledown.'

Off they went through the wood, and reached the cake shop at just exactly two o'clock.

The shop was empty, and Gubbleup knocked on the counter.

Nobody came. Gubbleup knocked more loudly. Still nobody came.

Then Gubbledown saw a note on the counter. On it was written:

Dear Gubbleup and Gubbledown,

I have to go out before two o'clock, but you will find your jellies and cakes in two big baskets under the counter.

From the Sugarstick Gnome.

The goblins ran round the counter to look for the baskets underneath. Sure enough, there they were.

Gubbleup stooped to get them, but he was so tall that he bumped against the kitchen door just behind him. It flew open. Gubbledown was just going to shut it, when he caught sight of something that made him stop.

He saw the magic currant all by itself in the middle of a plate on the kitchen table!

'Look! Look, Gubbleup!' he cried. 'There's the magic currant!'

They stared at it – and the same naughty idea crept into their minds.

'Shall we borrow it, just for today?' whispered Gubbleup. 'The Sugarstick Gnome's out, so we can't ask him if we may.'

'We'll ask him afterwards,' giggled Gubbledown. 'We'll take it back tonight and tell him we borrowed it. He can't say no then! We'll make a fine Christmas pudding for our party!'

The two rascally goblins picked up the currant, slammed the kitchen door, caught up their baskets and ran off.

'We'll give our guests such a surprise,' grinned Gubbleup. 'We'll let them see a Christmas pudding made before their eyes!'

The goblins hurriedly turned out the jellies

into pretty dishes, and spread out the cakes on their blue plates.

Right in the middle of the table they put a great big plate, and in the centre they placed the magic currant.

Soon the guests began to come, and very soon the party was in full swing. They played games and laughed until they were all out of breath.

'Now we'll have something to eat!' cried Gubbledown, leading the way into his bright little kitchen, where the meal was set out. Everyone took their places, and looked hungrily at the jellies, cakes and biscuits.

Then someone saw the empty plate on the table, with the little currant set in the middle.

'Whatever's that?' he cried.

Everybody looked. Gubbleup and Gubbledown laughed.

'Aha!' said Gubbleup. 'That's a great surprise for you all, when you've eaten up everything else!'

Well, everybody was most puzzled. They couldn't

think what the surprise could be, though they tried their very hardest. They ate up all the biscuits and cakes, finished the jellies and drank the lemonade.

Then they waited to see what the surprise was.

'Watch!' said Gubbleup.

Then he and Gubbledown danced solemnly round the table, and sang the magic song:

'Little black currant of mine,
Make me a pudding, I pray,
A Christmas pudding as fine
As anyone's baking today!'

And as before the currant seemed to swell and a little pudding began to grow on the plate. How everyone stared!

'My!' they cried. 'Good gracious! What a wonderful thing to be sure! A Christmas pudding growing before our eyes!'

'How do you stop it growing?' asked someone.

'That's easy!' said Gubbleup. 'You just take out the magic currant, and the pudding stops at once!'

The pudding went on getting bigger and bigger. Soon it was the size of a cricket ball, then of a melon, then of a football.

'We'll let it grow just a little bigger,' said Gubbleup. 'It does look such a nice one.'

They waited a minute longer, then they decided it was big enough.

Gubbleup bent over the pudding to take out the magic currant.

But oh dear me! All the currants looked exactly alike, and Gubbleup didn't know at all which was the one he wanted.

He picked out first one and then another – but he didn't get the right one, for still the pudding went on growing! He tried again, and Gubbledown helped him.

Not a bit of good! The pudding went on growing!

'Ha ha! Ho ho!' laughed everyone. 'We shall all be

able to have a great big helping, Gubbleup!'

The two goblins went on hurriedly picking out currants, hoping to come to the right one – and still the pudding went on growing.

It was bigger than the plate now, and little by little began to spread over the table. It grew as big as a pail – then as big as a dustbin, then as tall as a pillar box, but much wider.

The two goblins were getting frightened. Suppose they couldn't find the magic currant! Every minute was making it more difficult, for the pudding seemed to be getting fuller and fuller of currants!

The guests thought it was a fine joke. They thought Gubbleup and Gubbledown were giving them a great treat, and they longed to begin on the pudding.

'Yes, cut yourselves big slices!' said Gubbleup, suddenly thinking that the pudding would certainly be made smaller then. So everyone cut a huge slice and began eating.

But the pudding went on growing! Soon it reached

the ceiling, and was squashed down flat. But that made it grow wider, and it was soon bigger than the table.

Then bits fell on to the floor, and made a dreadful mess. The guests began to think something really must be wrong. They felt afraid.

'Can you really not stop the pudding growing?' asked one of them.

'No!' said Gubbleup, almost crying. 'Oh dear, oh dear, it will grow as big as this room, I do believe!'

'Gubbleup!' said Gubbledown in despair. 'Let's go and ask the Sugarstick Gnome to stop it for us!'

'You go,' said Gubbleup.

So off went Gubbledown and ran all the way. He burst into the shop, and to his great relief saw that the Sugarstick Gnome was home again.

The Sugarstick Gnome was looking terribly cross. He frowned when he saw Gubbledown.

'Did you take my magic currant?' he thundered.

'Yes, yes,' stammered Gubbledown, 'we – we b-b-borrowed it, and now we c-c-can't stop the p-p-pudding growing. Would you come and take the currant away?'

'No!' said the Sugarstick Gnome. 'You can keep it.'

'Oh please, please, please!' begged Gubbledown. 'The pudding will force our roof off, I do believe.'

'What will you give me if I come?' asked the Sugarstick Gnome.

'We haven't any money,' said Gubbledown, sadly.

'Well, will you both come and chop up firewood for me each day for a month?' asked the Sugarstick Gnome.

'Yes, yes, yes!' cried Gubbledown, 'But please do come now!'

The Sugarstick Gnome went off with him. When they came to Gubble Cottage they saw the pudding bulging out of the window. It was so big that everyone had had to go out of the room. Poor Gubbleup was terribly afraid the walls would be broken down.

The Sugarstick Gnome wriggled into the room,

and quick as a wink picked out a currant. At once the pudding stopped growing.

'Oh, thank you, thank you!' cried Gubbleup.

'You are two bad little goblins to borrow something without asking,' said the Sugarstick Gnome. 'I've a good mind to spank you both. Mind you come every day for a month and chop firewood for me as a punishment.'

He stalked off. All the guests said goodbye too, and went.

Gubbleup and Gubbledown stared at each other.

'The party's quite spoilt,' said Gubbleup, sadly.

'It's our own fault,' said Gubbledown miserably. 'But oh, Gubbleup – what are we to do with that great pudding filling up our kitchen like that?'

'Eat it, I suppose,' said Gubbleup.

The next day they went to chop firewood for the Sugarstick Gnome, and he kept them at it all the morning. For a month they worked for him, and very hard they found it.

But the horridest thing of all was eating the huge Christmas pudding. They got so tired of it that they vowed they would never touch another one all their lives long.

So if you ever meet two goblins who can't bear the sight of Christmas pudding, just ask them if their names are Gubbleup and Gubbledown!

The Wishing Glove

The Wishing Glove

PETER WAS looking out of the window on Christmas Eve. He was feeling very sad.

'It's going to be a *horrid* Christmas!' he said. 'No holly, no pudding, no presents!'

'Try not to mind so much, Peter,' said his mother. 'Daddy can't help being out of work, and it's just as bad for all your little brothers and sisters as for you.'

'Yes, I know,' said Peter. 'I'm not bothering about myself, Mother, truly I'm not – but I do so wish we could give Mollie and Peggie and Sandy and Jack a good time. Why, they haven't even got shoes to wear now! As for Daddy and you, I don't believe you've had enough to eat for weeks! And now it's Christmas!'

'Cheer up!' said his mother. 'Perhaps Santa Claus will remember us.'

Peter turned to the window again. He could see nothing but blackness – but suddenly he heard something. It was the sound of jingling bells. Nearer and nearer it came, nearer and nearer. Peter strained his eyes to see what sort of cart was coming by, but the night was too black.

Jingle – jingle – jingle, went the bells. *Jingle – jingle – jingle!*

Then something passed like a flash and was gone. Only the bells could still be heard in the distance.

'Now what in the wide world could that have been?' wondered Peter. 'I'll just pop outside and see if I can find out.'

He ran out into the snowy road and looked up and down. Nothing could be seen, but he could still faintly hear the bells.

He turned to go back, when suddenly his foot

knocked against something. He picked it up. It was large and heavy and soft, and Peter couldn't think *what* it could be.

'I'll take it indoors and see,' he decided. He ran into the house and looked at what he had found. It was an enormous furry glove!

'Good gracious!' said Peter, showing it to his mother. 'Look at this huge glove, Mother! Whoever could have dropped it?'

'It *is* big,' said his mother. 'Whoever owns it will be very sorry he has lost it.' Then she laughed. 'Perhaps it was Santa Claus, Peter!'

'Santa Claus!' said Peter – then he stood still and stared at his mother.

'I believe you're right!' he cried. 'Those jingling bells must have been reindeer bells! Oh Mother! Fancy finding Santa Claus's glove!'

He slipped the great thing on his right hand.

'Look, Mother!' he said. 'Isn't it lovely!'

His mother smiled at him. Then she shivered, for

she was very cold, and there was no fire.

'Oh, Mother!' said Peter, despairingly. 'I can't bear you to be cold. I do *wish* you had a nice warm shawl!'

Just as he spoke, a big red shawl appeared out of nowhere and draped itself warmly around his mother's shoulders!

Peter trembled with fright, and stared in amazement. His mother looked at the shawl open-mouthed. Neither of them spoke for a whole minute.

'Mother!' whispered Peter. 'Mother! You didn't have that shawl before, did you?'

'No,' whispered back his mother. 'Is it a trick you're playing, Peter?'

'No, no!' said Peter. 'I've never seen it before. It came suddenly out of the air, just as I was saying I wished you had a nice warm shawl.'

'Well, it certainly is a beauty,' said his mother, pulling it more closely around her. 'I haven't felt so cosy for weeks!'

Peter couldn't make it out. Then he suddenly

caught sight of the big fur glove on his right hand.

'Mother!' he cried. 'I believe this glove's a magic one! I believe it's because I'm wearing it that my wish came true! Shall I try another wish?'

'Yes,' said his mother, eagerly.

'I do wish we had a nice warm fire!' said Peter.

Immediately the hearth was filled with crackling wood, and great flames roared up the chimney, sending a warm glow all over the little room.

Peter and his mother stared in delight. As they looked, in came all the children to see what the crackling noise was.

'A fire! A fire!' they cried with joy and ran forward to warm their hands. 'Where did it come from, Mother?'

Their mother didn't answer. She was too astonished and delighted. Peter laughed aloud with gladness.

'I wish for a fine big loaf of bread and a jug of boiling milk!' he cried.

Clap, bang! On the table appeared an enormous

loaf and a jug of steaming milk.

'Ooh! Ooh! Look!' shrieked the children. 'Can we have some, Mother?'

'Yes, yes!' she cried. 'Sit down in front of the fire and I will make you bread and milk.'

In two minutes everyone was eating bread and milk by the roaring fire. The children could hardly believe it, and as for Peter, he had never felt so excited and so proud in his life.

He told the others how he had found the glove, and that he thought it must have been dropped by Santa Claus.

'That's why it's magic,' he cried. 'We can have anything we wish for!'

'Listen! Here's Daddy!' cried the children. 'Let's give him a surprise when he comes in, shall we? What shall we wish for?'

'Don't tell him about the magic glove!' said Peter. 'We'll just make him tremendously astonished!'

He thought for a moment. Then he wished.

'I wish that a joint of roast beef and roast potatoes were on the table,' he said. 'And I wish that a fine pair of warm slippers was by Daddy's chair!'

Immediately a joint of roast beef clapped itself on the table, surrounded by a crowd of delicious brown potatoes, all sitting in brown gravy. How glorious it smelt! All the children put their little noses in the air and sniffed hungrily.

By their father's chair appeared a pair of red fleecy slippers, ready to be popped on. The children pointed to them in glee, and were hushed by Peter, who heard his daddy coming up the stairs.

The footsteps were slow and heavy, and sounded tired. The door opened and in came their father, sad because he had brought nothing for Christmas Day.

Directly he saw the big red glow of the fire he stopped in amazement. Then he smelt the roast beef, and turned his eyes to the table. He opened them wider than ever, and then rubbed them hard.

'Roast beef and potatoes!' he cried, wonderingly.

'And warm slippers, Daddy!' shouted all the children, pointing under the chair.

Their father walked to the table as if he were in a dream, and sat down. Peter pulled off his boots for him, and put on the lovely warm slippers, while his mother cut off a great helping of beef, and piled potatoes on a plate.

'Where did they all come from?' asked the astonished man.

'Never mind, never mind!' laughed Peter. 'Just eat your supper, and then perhaps we'll tell you.'

His father began to eat hungrily and soon his plate was empty. Once again it was filled, and he started on his second helping.

'Where did you get it from?' he asked.

'We'll tell you soon, Daddy, we'll tell you soon!' laughed the children, thoroughly enjoying the secret.

At last their father's hunger was satisfied and he drew his chair up to the fire.

'Now tell me,' he cried, holding out his hands to the warm flames.

'Well, first of all, look at this glove!' said Peter, holding out his right hand. His father looked at it in surprise.

'Now watch!' said Peter. 'I wish we had a big plate of cakes here.'

Immediately a large plate of cakes appeared out of nowhere and stood on their father's lap. He was so astonished that he nearly fell off his chair.

'Bless my soul!' he cried. 'Where did the thing come from?'

He caught hold of the dish and held it. On it were about twenty fine fat cakes that seemed to cry out to be eaten.

Everybody took one, and soon there was such a munching going on that nobody spoke a word for quite five minutes.

Peter finished first.

'I wish Daddy had a watch!' he cried – and before

the surprised man could say anything, a brand-new watch clapped itself into his pocket.

'I wish Mother had a pair of fine shoes on her feet!' cried Peter.

At once his mother's old cracked shoes flew off, and a beautiful new pair flew on. The children shouted in delight, and their parents smiled and stared.

'Stop! Stop!' cried their father at last. 'Tell me the secret of all this, Peter.'

Peter told him.

'I found the glove out in the road,' he said, 'and it's a magic one. I'm sure I heard Santa Claus go by, so I think he must have dropped it. I brought it in, and we've been using it ever since. That's the secret, Daddy!'

His father looked as if he couldn't believe such a thing – but he knew it must be so. He thought for a few minutes, and then he spoke rather gravely.

'There's just one thing I'm wondering about,' he cried. 'And that is – ought we to use someone else's glove like this? For all we know, we may be using up all its magic, and the person it belongs to may be very angry.'

'Oh! Daddy!' cried Peter, taking off the glove. 'I never thought of that. Do you suppose it really matters?'

'I don't know,' said his father, uncomfortably. 'I think we ought to try and find the owner at once, and tell him what we've done. That's the fairest thing we can do. We can give back the shawl, the slippers and the watch.'

'But we can't give back the bread and milk and cakes and meat!' said Peter. 'I'm rather glad we can't, too – I did so enjoy them!'

'How can we find the owner, though?' asked his mother. 'Peter scarcely saw him, and it is only our guess that it is Santa Claus. We don't know where he is at all.'

The father laughed.

'That doesn't matter!' he said. 'We will just wish

him here! Put on the glove and wish, Peter.'

The boy slipped on the big glove.

'I wish that the owner of this glove were here,' he said.

Immediately loud footsteps were heard on the stairs, and the door was flung open.

In came a fat, jolly-looking man, dressed in a red tunic.

'Santa Claus, Santa Claus!' shouted the children.

'Hallo, hallo!' said Santa Claus. 'Did somebody use my wishing glove, and wish me here?'

'Yes, I did,' said Peter, nervously. 'I found it in the road, and used it for lots of things. I wished for a fire because we were cold, and a shawl for my mother, and meat for my daddy, and slippers and lots of things. Then Daddy thought you might be angry if we used up all the magic, so we wished for you to come!'

'Well, well!' said Santa Claus, taking his glove. 'I should have been annoyed, certainly, if you'd never told me – but as it is I'm most pleased that my old glove came in useful. I can't stop now, as Christmas Eve is my busiest night – but I shall come along again tonight when you're all in bed. So hang up your stockings, my dears, hang up your stockings!'

He laughed loudly, and ran down the stairs. Nobody spoke for a moment.

'Well, it was a good thing we owned up,' said Peter. 'I wonder if he really *will* come tonight!'

'Let's go to bed and hang up our stockings and see!' cried the children.

So they did, but although they tried their hardest to keep awake and see Santa Claus again, they didn't get a peep at him at all.

Still, they knew he had been, for you should have seen their stockings next morning! Nobody would have believed so many presents could have been crammed into such tiny stockings.

Even the cat had a present of a fine piece of red ribbon – so it's no wonder Peter's family believe in Santa Claus, is it?

Mr Icy-Cold

Mr Icy-Cold

ONCE UPON a time, one very snowy week, six children began to build a snowman. How hard they worked! You should have seen them, scraping the snow off the grass and off the top of the hedges, slapping it together to make the snowman's body, and patting it neatly into shape.

'This is fun!' said Mary.

'He will be the biggest snowman ever seen!' said Alan.

'I shall ask Mother to give me an old cap of Daddy's for him to wear,' said Rachel.

'Let's give him two feet, and put shoes on them so

that he can walk about if he wants to!' said John.

The others laughed. 'I *should* be astonished if I saw him walking down the garden!' said Ian.

'We'll call him Mr Icy-Cold!' said Gillian.

When they had finished the snowman it was three o'clock. 'Now we will dress him!' said Mary.

'He has a head as big as a giant's football!' said Alan.

'Here's Daddy's old cap for him!' said Rachel, running up with a big checked cap and putting it on the snowman's head. He did look splendid!

'And here are two old shoes belonging to Grandpa!' said John, putting them on the snowman's feet. It was difficult to put them on! John filled the shoes with snow, and then pushed them well under the snowman, so that they stuck out in a very realistic manner.

'He's going to walk, he's going to walk!' cried Ian.

'Come along indoors and have a nice hot drink of milk, Mr Icy-Cold!' shouted Gillian.

'He wouldn't like that,' said Mother, coming

up to look at the wonderful snowman. 'It would melt him inside!'

The children went in to tea. When the moon rose up in the sky, just about their bedtime, they looked out of the window and saw Mr Icy-Cold standing out there in the garden looking as real as could be. He wore Daddy's cap, he had an old pipe in his mouth, he had two great black eyes, he wore a ragged scarf round his neck, old gloves on his hands, and Grandpa's shoes. He really looked marvellous.

In the middle of the night a crowd of little snow-elves came flying up in their pretty sleigh, drawn by winter moths. When they saw Mr Icy-Cold they flew down to him at once.

'Oh!' they cried. 'A great big snowman! What is your name, Snowman?'

'I am Mr Icy-Cold,' said the snowman, in a soft snowy sort of voice. 'Come and talk to me.'

The snow-elves told him where they had come from – a land far away to the north, where there was always ice, always frost, always snow. The elves were pretty little creatures with frosty dresses, and wings as soft and as white as snow. Mr Icy-Cold liked them very much indeed. He felt lonely when they had gone. But they promised to come again the next night.

They kept their promise – but to Mr Icy-Cold's great dismay they were crying bitterly!

'What's the matter?' asked Mr Icy-Cold.

'Oh, two naughty pixies chased us, and broke our pretty sleigh. Look! It's no use now! We can't use it any more. We don't know what to do because when the weather turns warm, we must fly away to our own country of ice and snow. If we stay here when it is warm, we feel ill and fade away.'

Mr Icy-Cold was very sorry to hear all this.

'Where do those two pixies live?' he asked. 'I will go to them and make them mend your sleigh for you, or else give you a new one.'

'But snowmen can't walk!' cried the snow-elves.

'Oh, *can't* they?' said Mr Icy-Cold, and he laughed. 'Look!'

He stepped forward on his two big feet, and the elves cried out in surprise, for they had never seen a snowman walk before. He plodded down the garden and back, his two big shoes leaving footprints behind him.

'There you are!' he said. 'What did I tell you? Now where do those two naughty pixies live? I'll go and give them the fright of their lives!'

'Come with us and we'll show you,' said the elves, and dragging their broken sleigh behind them, they took the snowman down the garden, through a gate at the bottom, and into a field. The field sloped up into a hill, and in the middle of the hill was a little door.

'This is where the pixies live,' said the elves, half-frightened. Mr Icy-Cold knocked at the door softly. As soon as it was opened by the two pixies, the snowman reached out his big gloved hand and caught hold of them.

'Ooh! Ow! Ooh!' yelled the pixies, in a fright. 'Here's a big white giant! Ooh! Let us go!'

'You broke the sleigh belonging to the snow-elves!' said the snowman sternly. 'What are you going to do about it?'

'Oh, we'll mend it; oh, do let us go! We promise to mend it!' squealed the pixies. Mr Icy-Cold put them down on the ground, and looked at them sternly out of his big black stone eyes.

'Do it at once, or I'll carry you off with me!' he said. The pixies took the broken sleigh and looked at it. One of them fetched hammer and nails and screws. The other brought a few pieces of wood. Soon the night air was filled with the sound of hammering. Every now and again the two pixies stared round in fear at the big snowman, and he frowned as hard as he could.

'Get on with your job!' he said. So they hurried and hurried. The wind blew chill and Jack Frost was out and about. The pixies were cold and wanted to get back into their warm little house. Soon the sleigh was mended, and the snow-elves got into it with glad shouts and cries.

'Don't you dare to interfere with the snow-elves again!' said Mr Icy-Cold, and off he shuffled back to his place in the garden. The snow-elves went with him, making a great fuss of him, and telling him he was their best friend.

After that the elves and the snowman talked together every night. But soon the weather changed and the air became warm. The snow-elves began to think about going back to their own country of ice and snow.

'But how lonely I shall be without you!' said Mr Icy-Cold sadly. 'I shall stand here, thinking of you, all the spring and summer through, until the winter comes again and brings you with it.'

'No, Mr Icy-Cold, you won't stay here all the spring and the summer,' said the elves. 'You will melt. You will melt right away, and there will be nothing of you left when we come back next winter.'

Mr Icy-Cold stared at the elves in horror, and his stone eyes seemed to get bigger and bigger.

'Melt!' he said. 'Did you say I shall melt? Won't there be anything left of me?'

'Not a thing,' said the elves sadly. 'That's the worst of being a snowman, you know. You only last whilst the snow and ice are here. Then you disappear for ever.'

Nobody spoke for a minute. Mr Icy-Cold was too upset, and the elves too sad. Then a small elf gave a little squeal and made everybody jump.

'I've got an idea, I've got an idea!' she cried. 'Why shouldn't Mr Icy-Cold come back to our land with us! It's always cold and frosty there, and snow is always on the ground. He would never melt there. He would be able to live with us for ever!'

'Of course, of course!' shouted the snow-elves in delight. 'You must start tonight, Mr Icy-Cold. We will make our winter moths fly very slowly, and you must follow us carefully. Come now, this very minute – for the weather is getting warmer, and if you begin to melt you may not be able to walk!'

So Mr Icy-Cold followed the little sleigh, drawn by moths, and plodded on and on and on towards the north. He went over fields and hills, down lanes and high roads, and the elves always found a good place to hide him in the daytime.

Once the weather got a bit too warm, and the snowman's nose melted a bit. But the next night was frosty again, so he was all right. And at last he got to the land of the snow-elves. He was safe!

'Welcome to our home!' cried the snow-elves, kissing him on his cold cheek. 'You shall build yourself a little snow house with windows and a door, and do just whatever you like.'

The six children who had built the snowman were most surprised to find him gone.

'Oh, he's just melted,' said Mother.

'But, Mother, his cap, and his scarf, and his gloves

and his shoes can't have melted too!' said Mary. 'It's most mysterious! I wonder where he is, funny old Mr Icy-Cold?'

He was building himself a little house in the land of the snow-elves, as happy as could be! And there he lives to this day, still wearing the same old cap and the same old shoes – funny Mr Icy-Cold!

The Fairies'
Christmas Party

The Fairies'
Christmas Party

EMMA'S TOYS all lived in a big wooden cupboard in the playroom. There were four dolls, a teddy bear, a big panda, an elephant, two bunnies, a Jack-in-the-box, a postman and a dog. There was a box of wooden bricks, a dolls' house, a tea set and a lovely musical box that Emma had been given for her birthday.

Of all her toys, Emma loved her musical box best. When she turned the handle it played six different tunes that you could dance to. Emma played it every single day – and her toys played it at night! At least, Braces the teddy bear played it because he was the strongest and could go on turning the handle for a long time while the toys danced round the playroom.

One cold, frosty night, a pixie flew to the window and looked in. She saw the toys dancing, while Braces turned the handle on the musical box. She thought it was a lovely sight, so she jumped down from the windowsill, took hold of the panda and danced round the playroom with him.

After that she often came to the playroom to listen to the musical box and to join in the dancing. It was great fun.

'I shan't be coming tomorrow night,' she told them one evening. 'It is Christmas Eve and the Fairy Queen is holding a dance at the bottom of the garden. We are going to have a band from Dreamland to play for us – a wonderful band that can play dance music better than any other band in the world!'

'We'll peep out of the window and see if we can hear it,' promised Braces.

So, on Christmas Eve, the toys all leant out of

the window to hear the band, but although they listened and listened they couldn't hear a thing!

They were wondering what could have happened, when the little pixie came flying up to the window quite out of breath.

'Oh dear,' she said, 'what do you think has happened? Why, the Dreamland band has made a mistake. They thought the queen's dance was tomorrow, instead of tonight – and they haven't come!'

'What are you going to do?' asked the teddy bear. 'Have all the guests arrived?'

'Yes, all of them!' said the pixie. 'And there is no music for them to dance to. Isn't it dreadful?'

'Dreadful!' agreed the toys, shaking their heads. But what could be done?

Then the teddy bear had a marvellous idea. 'I say!' he cried. 'What about the musical box? You could dance to that, and I could come and turn the handle for you!'

'Ooh! What a good idea!' cried the pixie, delighted.

'The queen will be so pleased, and all the guests will think the musical box is wonderful!'

'Well, we will have to ask Emma first if she will lend it to us,' said Braces to the pixie. 'You see, the musical box belongs to her, and she is very fond of it. I am sure it isn't right to borrow things belonging to other people unless you ask them first. Shall I go and ask her?'

'Let's all go!' said the big panda.

So the toys crept along the darkened hallway, up the stairs and into the bedroom where Emma lay fast asleep, dreaming dreams of Christmas.

Braces hopped up on to the bed and shook her gently. She awoke with surprise and sat up, rubbing her eyes.

'Don't be frightened,' said Braces. 'It's only your toys, and a little pixie. We've come to ask if we could borrow your musical box, just for tonight? The Fairy Queen is giving a Christmas dance and the band hasn't come.'

'Good gracious! Have all you toys come to life?' cried Emma, in surprise.

'Shh! Don't wake the grown-ups,' said Braces. 'Yes, we toys always come to life at night, Emma. But what about your beautiful musical box? Please may we borrow it? Just for tonight.'

'Of course!' said Emma, 'I would be delighted to lend it for a fairy dance – but who will turn the handle?'

'I will,' said Braces. 'I always turn the handle because my arms are strong and they don't get tired.'

'What fun!' said Emma. 'Oh, look at this dear little pixie! Are you real?'

'Of course I am!' said the pixie, laughing. 'Thank you so much for lending us the musical box. We promise to look after it.'

They ran out of the bedroom, leaving Emma to fall asleep again, this time dreaming of pixies and teddy bears that could walk and talk.

'Who will carry the musical box?' asked the panda

when they were all back in the playroom. 'It is very heavy!'

The toys thought about it for a while and then Braces asked the strong wooden horse if he could manage to carry it in his cart down to the end of the garden. He said he could, so off they all went, out through the playroom window.

It was cold out in the garden and a fluffy layer of snow covered the grass. The light from a silvery moon and a thousand twinkling stars lit their way and made the garden look so beautiful that the toys thought they had reached Fairyland.

Very soon they arrived at the place where the dance was supposed to be, under the shelter of a big fir tree. The Fairy Queen was there, looking very disappointed, and all the guests were wondering what to do.

They were most surprised to see the toys, but the little pixie lost no time in explaining why they had come.

The queen was delighted to hear about the musical

box. Then Braces and the big panda lifted it out of the cart and Braces started to turn the handle.

The tinkling music began and soon all the fairy folk were dancing merrily, round and round beneath the branches of the old tree. All the toys danced too, and the panda even danced with the Fairy Queen herself!

At midnight, everyone sat down and had a delicious feast. There were fairy cakes, cups of tasty nectar and soft sweets made from honey. The toys wanted the party to go on for ever. They had never had such a good time in all their lives!

When the first light of dawn tinged the sky, the fairies said it was time for them to leave. The toys knew that they too should go, back to the playroom, for it would soon be daylight.

'Well, thank you very much indeed,' said the Fairy Queen. 'Your musical box certainly made our Christmas party a great success. It was kind of you to lend it to me.'

'Oh, Emma lent it – we didn't,' said Braces, and he

told the queen all about the little girl and how they had woken her up to ask about the musical box. 'She is really very kind and good to us,' he said.

'Well, it was very kind of her,' said the Fairy Queen. 'I must send a letter to thank her.' And, taking out a tiny sheet of paper and a beautiful silver pen, she wrote a little letter and tucked it into Braces' pocket. She said goodbye and wished them all a Merry Christmas. Then she drove away in her golden carriage with the Fairy King by her side.

The toys stood and waved until the queen's carriage had disappeared in the distance. All the fairies, except for the little pixie, had left with her.

'I must go, too,' said the pixie. 'And you must go home. Thank you so much for helping us.' And with that she flew away, after the Fairy Queen.

'Merry Christmas!' cried the toys after her. 'Come and see us again soon!'

When Emma woke up she quite forgot at first that it was Christmas Day. All she could think about was how her toys had come to life the night before. She ran to the playroom to ask them about it – but they were all sitting very still and quiet. They could not speak or move because now it was daytime.

Emma began to wonder if it had all been a dream. She went back to her bedroom and looked in her Christmas stocking – and what do you think she found? Right on top of all her presents was a tiny letter, written in the most perfect handwriting! Emma pulled it out and opened it. It said:

Dear Emma,

Thank you very much for lending us your lovely musical box. Will you please come to our next dance, when the moon is full, and bring your musical box again? The Fairy King says he would love to dance with you.

Have a very Merry Christmas.

Love from

The Fairy Queen

Well, Emma could hardly believe her eyes! Would she go? Of course she would, and the moon will soon be full again so she won't have to wait too long, will she?

The Christmas Party

The Christmas Party

DONALD WAS a lonely boy, for he had no brothers or sisters, and instead of going to school his mother taught him his lessons. So he had no friends and no one to play with. And will you believe it, he had never been asked to a party in his life!

At Christmas time he used to peep into other people's windows and see the children dancing round the Christmas tree and pulling crackers. He did so long to join them, but no one ever asked him.

One day, just after Christmas, Donald dressed himself up in the Wild West clothes that his mother had given him for Christmas. He looked very fine in the leather tunic, fringed trousers and enormous feathered headdress. Just as he had finished dressing he looked out of the window and saw that there was a party next door. It was a fancy dress party too! All the children that arrived were dressed up as fairies, clowns, milkmaids or soldiers.

I'll go and watch them arriving, thought Donald. *That will be fun.* So he slipped out of his front door and watched the children arrive. When they had all come he saw them playing games in the front room. So he went over to their front gate and watched.

Presently the door opened and a lady ran down to the gate. She took Donald's hand and pulled him to the door. 'Here's a late little boy!' she called. 'He's too shy to come in. Look at his beautiful fancy dress!'

Donald tried to explain that he hadn't been asked to the party, but nobody listened to him. Soon he found himself playing musical chairs and pass the parcel, and then, dear me, he was sitting down to a most glorious tea! After that there was a conjuror who made a rabbit come out of Donald's tunic and two pennies out of his ears! Then there was a wonderful Christmas tree and Donald was given a fine trumpet and a box of chocolates.

All the other children liked Donald. He was full of fun, he didn't push or snatch, and he was just as ready to pass cakes at teatime as to take them. The grown-ups liked him too, for he had good manners. As for Donald, he had never been so happy in his entire life.

But the loveliest thing of all was when the prizes were given! Who do you think won the first prize for the best fancy dress costume? Yes, Donald!

'But I can't take it,' he said. 'I wasn't asked to this party, really. That lady over there pulled me in. I'm only the little boy from next door, and this is the first party I've ever been to!'

'Well, of all the funny things!' cried the grown-ups. 'We wondered who you were! But never mind, little boy, you deserve the first prize, so here it is – a railway train! And we hope you'll often come here and play with these children again.'

Donald ran straight home with his prize, and his mother was astonished!

'I shan't be lonely any more!' said Donald. And you may be sure he wasn't.

Pins and Needles!

Pins and Needles!

QUICK-FINGERS, the pixie dressmaker, was chased one night by the red goblin. She ran through the fields panting and a small bush called to her. 'Quick-Fingers, hide beneath me! I will shelter you!'

So Quick-Fingers crawled under the small bush and stayed there safely till the morning. She slept quite soundly, though it rained. But the bush held its leaves over her and not one drop of rain wetted the pixie's frock.

She awoke to hear a munching, crunching sound. 'Oh dear, oh dear!' the little bush said. 'Here's that great donkey again, eating me as fast as he can. I shall never grow, I shall never grow. As soon as I clothe myself with fresh green leaves, along comes the donkey or the horse or the sheep; they munch and nibble at me all day long!'

The pixie was sorry for the little bush. She took out a needle and spoke to the donkey. 'Donkey, stop eating this bush! If you don't, I'll prick you with my needle!'

The donkey didn't stop, so he got pricked. He brayed and ran away. The little bush was surprised that he had gone so quickly.

'What did you use to prick him with? What have you got in that box there?'

'Pins and needles,' said Quick-Fingers. 'Oh, little bush, if only you grew pins and needles round your leaves nobody would ever come to eat you!'

'Do you know enough magic to grow me some?' asked the bush eagerly.

'I think so,' said Quick-Fingers. 'I'll set pins and needles all round the edges of some of your leaves and sing a magic spell over them. Then they will grow and all your new leaves will grow pins and needles too!'

'Oh, thank you,' said the bush, 'then no one will ever want to come and eat me!'

The pixie did as she had said and then she sang a little spell. She said goodbye and went. 'I'll come back in a month and see how the magic has worked,' she promised.

When she came back, what a difference there was in the bush! It had grown well, for no one had dared to eat it.

Every leaf was set with prickles, as sharp as needles, as strong as pins!

'The donkey doesn't come near me! The horse is afraid of me! The sheep keep as far away as they can!' said the bush joyfully. 'Now I can grow big. I can grow into a high tree.'

'Well, mind you don't waste your pins and needles if you grow tall,' said the pixie. 'No animal can eat your high-up leaves, so you needn't bother about pins and needles for them.'

Do you know what the tree is?

Guess! Yes, it's the prickly holly tree, and you've all seen how well its leaves are set with pins and needles!

And do you know, the tree took Quick-Fingers' advice and didn't grow prickles on its top leaves.

That's strange, isn't it? But if you'll look and see, you'll find it's true.

Mr Loud-Voice
Makes a Mistake

Mr Loud-Voice Makes a Mistake

TICK AND TOCK lived in a little cottage down Lonely Lane, and although they worked very hard they hardly ever had much money.

'It's Christmas soon,' said Tick. 'Do let's try and save some money, Tock. We didn't have a plum pudding last year, or the Christmas before that either!'

'Well, if people would pay us what they owe us we should have quite enough money to have a plum pudding – *and* a nice fat goose – *and* to buy a present for one another,' said Tock.

'I wish Mr Loud-Voice would pay us what he owes!' said Tick. 'He owes us more than anyone else.

Now take little Mrs Gentle – *she's* paid us – and so has Mr Kindly.'

'Perhaps people with loud voices don't pay their bills!' said Tock. 'Listen, Mr Loud-Voice walks down our lane each evening – let's watch out for him today and ask him politely to pay our bill.'

So they watched for Mr Loud-Voice to come along with his yappy little dog, and when they saw him they ran out to him.

'Good evening, Mr Loud-Voice,' they said. 'We wish you a Merry Christmas when it comes – and please will you pay our bill? We do want a plum pudding for Christmas.'

'I'll pay your bill when I think I will!' said Mr Loud-Voice, booming at them angrily. 'How dare you rush at me like this and demand money! I never heard of such a thing! I'll set my dog on you if you dare to say another word!'

'But – but,' began Tick, upset – but he got no further because Mr Loud-Voice boomed at his dog,

'Go for them, Yap, go for them!'

Poor Tick and Tock had to run into their cottage at top speed or they would have been bitten. They slammed the door and stamped their feet.

'Hateful fellow!' said Tick. 'He *might* pay us a *little* of the money. He knows Christmas is coming. After all, we did work well for him!'

'Well – we shall have to make up our minds to go without goose and pudding,' said Tock, gloomily. 'What a horrid fellow Mr Loud-Voice is!'

Now next day it snowed. It snowed and it snowed and it snowed. Tick and Tock liked the snow and they thought it would be fun to build a snowman to amuse the passers-by.

'Come on – we'll build a beauty,' said Tick. 'The snow is just right to make a snowman.'

Well, they did build a fine one – big, tall, and very solid. They were very pleased with him indeed. When Mrs Gentle came by she laughed to see it. 'If you call at my cottage I'll give you my husband's old hat,' she said. 'And I think he's got a pair of old boots he won't wear again. Your snowman will like them.'

'Oh thank you,' said Tock, pleased. 'I'll go and fetch them at once, Mrs Gentle.'

On the way back with the old hat and shoes, he met Mr Kindly and told him about the snowman.

'Ah – he needs to wear more than a hat and shoes,' said Mr Kindly. 'He needs a coat and a scarf. You come in with me and I'll give you my old mackintosh and a red scarf – and maybe a stick.'

So, when Tock arrived back at his cottage, he had a hat, scarf, coat, stick and boots for the snowman. Tick was very pleased.

'Mr Very-Cold will be glad of these!' he said. 'Won't you, snowman? Help me to dress him, Tock.'

The snowman looked very, very real indeed when Tick and Tock had finished with him. 'He looks as if he is just about to walk away!' said Tick. 'Well, it's getting dark now, Mr Very-Cold, so we'll leave you and go and warm ourselves by our fire. Good night!'

'And don't you let Mr Loud-Voice be rude to you when he comes along!' said Tock.

Well, of course, Mr Loud-Voice came along as usual, and didn't see the snowman till he was almost on top of him. It made him jump.

'Hey – get out of my way – standing there in the dark like that!' said Mr Loud-Voice. 'Who are you, I'd like to know, blocking up half the footpath?'

The snowman said nothing. Mr Loud-Voice could only just see him in the starlight, and he felt sure that the snowman was grinning rudely at him.

'If you don't apologise and get out of my way at once, I'll knock your hat off!' cried Mr Loud-Voice, raising his stick. 'And set my dog on you too. Here, Yap – go for him!'

Tick and Tock heard all the noise and came out to see what was happening. Shouting and barking – goodness, it could only be Mr Loud-Voice!

They were just in time to see Yap, the dog, fly at the snowman and bite his mackintosh coat – and they saw

Mr Loud-Voice striking at him with his stick, meaning to knock off his hat.

But he struck off the whole of Mr Very-Cold's snow head – and there he stood, with no head at all! Mr Loud-Voice hadn't expected that, of course, and he had a really dreadful shock!

'Ooooh!' he said. 'I've knocked off his head. But I didn't mean to – no, I didn't mean to!'

'You wicked man!' said Tick, coming up. 'Just see what you've done to our good friend, Mr Very-Cold. Poor, poor fellow – he's got no head now.'

'Don't fetch the police!' begged Mr Loud-Voice. 'The fellow was rude to me – wouldn't get out of my way. He – he struck out at me and I just tried to hit his hat off – that's all. Really it is. How was I to know his head would fly off!'

'*Shall* we fetch the police, Tock?' asked Tick, trying not to laugh. 'We could tell them about the money that Mr Loud-Voice owes us then.'

'No, no – don't get the police, I tell you!' shouted

Mr Loud-Voice. 'Here – look, take my purse, and all the money in it and keep it for what I owe you. But please, please don't call the police!'

Tick took the purse at once, and then Mr Loud-Voice and the dog took to their heels and fled down the lane as fast as they could go. Tick and Tock laughed till the tears ran down their cheeks. Oh dear, oh dear – to think that Mr Loud-Voice hadn't guessed that Mr Very-Cold was only a snowman!

They put Mr Very-Cold's head on again and went indoors to see what was in the purse. 'My goodness me!' said Tick. 'There's twice as much money here as he owes us!'

'Let's take what we ought to have – and we'll give him the rest back tomorrow, and tell him that Mr Very-Cold was only a snowman!' said Tock, with a laugh.

But Mr Loud-Voice never came down the lane again. He was so shocked at what he had done that he packed his things that very night, and took the first train he could catch, which went to the Land of Never-Come-Back.

So Tick and Tock found themselves quite rich, and had a fat goose and a most enormous pudding on Christmas Day. They asked Mrs Gentle and Mr Kindly, of course – and how they wished they could ask Mr Very-Cold too! Still, they gave him a pipe to smoke, and he was very very pleased with that!

'What's Happened
to Michael'?

'What's Happened to Michael'?

'I'VE GOT four shillings and threepence saved up for Christmas presents already,' said Jane, counting out coins from her money box.

'I've got three shillings exactly,' said Peter. 'I had to give a shilling in at school for Miss Brown's wedding present. How much have *you* got, Michael?'

'Not much,' said Michael, and he shook his money box out on the table. A penny and a threepenny bit rolled out. 'Fourpence! But I just can't bother to save!'

'I think you're mean,' said Jane. 'You never save up to buy people birthday presents or Christmas presents.

You just give them old toys of yours. You spend all your money on yourself, and you don't try to earn any to save up, as we do!'

'He's lazy,' said Peter. 'He won't put himself out for anyone. Will you, Michael? You'll let us spend our saved-up money to buy you a Christmas present – but you wouldn't dream of doing the same for us.'

'Oh, be quiet,' said Michael. 'We can't all be the same. I don't want to bother to earn money, and I don't want to bother to save. You like it and I don't.'

He went out of the room and banged the door.

'He really is mean,' said Jane. 'He never even bought Mummy a birthday present on her last birthday. He just went and picked some flowers out of the garden for her.'

'Well – I don't expect he'll ever be different,' said Peter. 'He just doesn't care.'

'There's one good thing about him though,' said Jane. 'He never borrows from us. Not like Tina at school, who's always borrowing something or other.'

'And he'd never dream of taking any money that belonged to anyone else,' said Peter. 'Like that horrid little James at school. *He* took Harry's bus money, you know – out of his desk. John saw him and made him put it back.'

'Yes – thank goodness Michael isn't a borrower or a stealer,' said Jane. 'He's just careless, and rather mean. He hardly ever gives anyone a present.'

Michael was out in the garden, looking for a ball he had lost. He thought of Jane and Peter and the money in their money boxes. He scowled to himself. All this fuss about saving up money to spend on other people! Birthdays and Christmases were a nuisance. There were quite enough things to buy without having to go and spend money on presents!

I've got fourpence – and as far as I can see that's about all I shall *have to spend at Christmas time on Mummy and Daddy and Jane and Peter*, thought Michael, hunting under the bushes for his ball. *A penny for each of them. I'll get them a card between them.*

Next day Mummy came into the playroom where the three children were reading. 'Will one of you go down to the village for me and fetch me some buns for tea?' she said. 'I meant to make some and I haven't had time.'

'I'll go,' said Michael. 'I've got to fetch my bike. It's at Fred's. I lent it to him.'

'Very well,' said his mother. 'Here is a shilling, Michael. Choose six nice buns. And will you go to the milk shop next door to the baker's and pay the bill for me? Here it is. Exactly ten shillings. I'll give you a ten-shilling note for it. Put the shilling and the note carefully into your purse. Bring back the bill with you, and see that the girl receipts it, so that I know it's paid.'

'Right, Mummy,' said Michael, and took the shilling and the ten-shilling note. He felt in his pocket for his purse, but it wasn't there. Bother! Where was it? Well, he would put the money into his pocket just as it was. He wouldn't have it there long!

He put on his hat and coat and went out, whistling. It was snowing hard, and he was pleased. He liked going out in the snow. Big snowflakes fell down all round him. He looked up into the heavy sky. Thousands of flakes were falling silently down and down and down. They gave him a pleasant but rather strange feeling.

He shuffled through the snow to his front gate. Then out into the road he went. He fetched his bike from Fred's first, but he couldn't ride it because already the snow was thick. He wheeled it to the baker's and stood looking into the shop. What buns should he buy? There were three different kinds. He would get two of each.

In he went and the girl put six buns into a paper bag. He gave her the shilling and went out to his bike. Now, what else did Mummy say he was to do? Oh yes – pay the milk bill. He felt in his pocket for the bill and pulled it out. It was ten shillings. He would give in the ten-shilling note, watch the girl write *Received with thanks* across the bill and go home. Tomorrow he would make Jane and Peter come into the garden and build a snowman.

He went into the milk shop. He felt in his pocket for the ten-shilling note. It wasn't there! He scrabbled hurriedly in all his pockets, one after another – but he couldn't find that note!

He went out of the shop before the girl came to serve him. He was very upset. What had happened to that ten shillings? It was a lot of money. He felt in all his pockets again, very, very carefully. But, quite certainly, the ten-shilling note wasn't there. Michael emptied out his pockets, laying everything on the top of the snow-covered wall nearby. String. Two toffees. A small ball. A pencil. A rubber. A big marble. But no ten-shilling note.

I've dropped it somewhere, thought Michael, and he went back to the baker's. No, he hadn't dropped it there. The shop was empty, and there was nothing on the floor. There was nothing in the snow outside, either.

'The snow must have covered it,' said Michael. 'I dropped it somewhere and the snow hid it. Blow, bother, blow! A whole ten-shilling note. Mummy will be awfully upset. I know she's saving up for Christmas, too – for crackers and balloons and things.'

He wheeled his bicycle home, feeling very miserable. Mummy had told him to put the note in his purse. It was so easy to lose loose money. What should he say to her? If she told Daddy, Michael would be sent to bed. Daddy didn't like carelessness with other people's money.

I can't even give Mummy anything out of my money box to make up for losing the ten shillings, thought Michael. *I've only got fourpence.*

He wheeled his bicycle up the hill to his house, thinking hard. 'Suppose I try and earn some money – perhaps I might even get ten shillings if I tried! Then I could go and pay the milk bill and nobody would know I'd lost Mummy's money. The milk shop won't send the bill in again for another week, so I've got a week. I could try, anyway. It would be difficult, I expect, to earn such a lot of money.'

He put his bicycle away and went indoors. He was met by his mother, who held out her hand for the buns. 'Put my milk bill receipt in my desk, Michael,' she said. 'What nice buns! Tea will be ready in five minutes. Tell the others, dear.'

Michael went to tell Jane and Peter. They were still counting their money and making out Christmas lists of presents. 'I haven't got enough money yet,' said Jane. 'I must somehow earn two shillings more.'

'I must get a bit more too,' said Peter. 'Hallo, Michael. You've been ages.' Michael looked at the little piles of money and wished he had as much. 'How are you going to earn any more?' he asked.

'Well, I know what *I* shall do,' said Peter. 'I shall dig away the snow from people's front paths. They always pay for that.'

'And I shall go and ask Mrs Johns if she wants me to take her two little children for a walk in the afternoons,' said Jane. 'And I could ask Auntie Nora if she wants any errands running. She knows I'm saving up for Christmas and she pays me a penny a time. I've told her I'll always do her errands for nothing if I'm not saving up.'

Michael made up his mind to go and ask Granny if she wanted any errands running. And he would take his spade and broom and do a little snow-moving too! And what about cleaning Uncle Dick's car? Uncle Dick had once said jokingly that he would give the children half a crown if any of them would like to clean his car. But it was such a big job that no one had taken it on.

Nobody could make out what had happened to Michael over the next few days. He shovelled snow away from this house and that house. He ran all Granny's errands quickly and well. He appeared at Uncle Dick's house and asked if he could clean the car.

'Half a crown to you if you do it well,' said Uncle Dick, pleased to see that it was Michael who had offered to do it. He had always thought that Michael was the lazy one of the three.

Mummy was astonished to hear what Michael was doing. Granny praised him and said how good and quick he was. Uncle Dick said he had never had his car cleaned so well, and he gave Michael three shillings instead of half a crown. Mrs Brown and Miss Toms told Mummy how well Michael had shovelled the snow from their front doors.

'What's *happened* to Michael?' she said, in wonder. The other two children said the same, two or three times a day. 'What's happened to Michael? He must be saving up for Christmas after all! He's earning a lot of money! We'll get presents from him if we're lucky.'

Michael didn't say he was saving up for Christmas, because he wasn't. He was trying to earn money to pay for the milk bill, to make up for the ten shillings he had lost. He emptied his money box one night and counted out what he had got.

'Half a crown. Two separate shillings. Five sixpences. Three threepenny bits, counting the one I had before. A two-shilling bit, and seven pennies, counting in the one I had before. Now, let's add them all up.'

Have *you* added them up? You have? Well, then, you know what they come to – ten shillings and fourpence! What a lot of money!

'Now I can pay that milk bill,' said Michael, pleased. And just at that very minute in came his mother. She held something in her hand.

'Look, Michael,' she said. 'I was sending your old blazer to the cleaners and I went through the pockets. There was a hole in one pocket and this had slipped through it and was down in the lining – a ten-shilling note! Where *did* you get it?'

Michael stood and stared at the note. Good gracious! So he *hadn't* lost it after all – it had slipped down into the lining. There it was!

'Oh, Mummy,' he said. 'I'll tell you what happened. I should have told you before, I know. You gave me that note to pay the milk bill – and I thought I had lost it; I didn't know it had slipped down into the lining. So I couldn't pay the bill and I've been hard at work earning money all this week to pay the milk bill myself. And now look at what I've earned! I've got ten shillings and fourpence in my money box!'

'Oh, Mike!' said his mother, astonished. 'You should have told me at once and I would have looked in the lining and found the note. But as it is you've now got this note to pay the bill – and all that money besides!'

'To spend on Christmas presents,' said Michael. 'Yes, that's what I shall do. I've saved up like the others – and I'll make a fine Christmas list!'

Well, he did. He put down all the names of the people he wanted to give presents to, and beside the names he put the things he meant to buy. What a wonderful day of shopping he would have – and how pleased everyone would be with their presents! They were, of course – and it was very nice for Michael to hear their thanks. It was the happiest Christmas he had ever had. But wasn't it funny that a ten-shilling note should cause all that?

Mr Widdle's Christmas Stocking

Mr Widdle's Christmas Stocking

MR WIDDLE was always excited when Christmas came near. He did love putting up the holly. He did love stirring the Christmas pudding. He did love hanging up his great big stocking on Christmas Eve.

'Ooooh! It is exciting!' said Mr Widdle, rubbing his hands together in glee, whenever he thought of all these things.

Now the postman kept coming to Mr Widdle's house and bringing most exciting parcels – at least, they *looked* exciting from the outside. Mrs Widdle used to pop them away in a cupboard of hers and wouldn't let Mr Widdle get so much as a peep at them!

But Mr Widdle didn't mind. He thought to himself, *All the more presents for my Christmas stocking! My word, it will be a fine stocking this year. It will take me a long time to get to the bottom of it. What fun!*

When Christmas Eve came Mr Widdle hung up his biggest stocking. My goodness, it *was* a big one, too – for Mr Widdle had very fat legs, and his stockings were very wide indeed! It kept slipping off the bed knob, so Mr Widdle scratched his head and wondered what to do.

'I'll tie it on with my garter,' said Mr Widdle. But even that didn't keep the stocking hanging up. So Mr Widdle looked round for something else and he thought his tie would do nicely to bind the top of the big stocking to the brass bed knob. So he tied it very tightly in three different knots and the stocking hung there beautifully, all ready to be filled.

Well, Mr Widdle fell so sound asleep that he wouldn't have heard a dozen Santa Clauses scrambling about the chimney! And in the morning, when he woke up, the first thing he thought was, *Christmas morning! Goody, goody! Now for my stocking!*

He looked eagerly down at the bottom of the bed – but to his great astonishment he could see no stocking there! He rubbed his eyes and looked again. No, there was no stocking there at all.

Well – no one had remembered him then! Santa Claus had forgotten him. Mrs Widdle had forgotten him. None of his friends had remembered him. He was a lonely and miserable man without a Christmas stocking, and everything was perfectly horrid.

Mr Widdle could hear Mrs Widdle getting the breakfast ready downstairs. He thought he had better get up or the sausages he could smell would be cold. So up he got, dressed himself, and went downstairs.

'Merry Christmas!' said Mrs Widdle, brightly. Mr Widdle made no answer, and Mrs Widdle looked up in great surprise. 'What's the matter?' she asked, when she saw Widdle's long face.

'I've had no Christmas stocking,' said Mr Widdle, gloomily.

'Rubbish!' said Mrs Widdle. 'I saw it myself this morning. Come along upstairs.'

So they went upstairs and Mrs Widdle laughed. 'Look!' she said, 'your stocking was *so* full and *so* heavy that it broke from the bed knob and fell on the floor! I suppose you didn't even *think* of looking there, Mr Widdle?'

'Oh!' said Mr Widdle, staring at the full stocking in delight. 'But look – my nice tie is split! The stocking has broken it.'

'Look inside the stocking and you may find a new one,' said Mrs Widdle. 'You *are* an old silly, aren't you!'

And he certainly was!

Who Could It Be?

'Who Could It Be?'

IT ALL began one afternoon when Sam and Valerie went home through the woods. It was a frosty December day, and the grass crunched under their feet as they walked.

'It sounds like toast!' said Valerie. 'Oh, Sam – aren't the woods lovely today! I do wish I was an artist – I'd sit down and paint that scene over there, look – with the bare trees, and the frozen pond, and the sun going down low in a red sky.'

'You wouldn't,' said Sam. 'Your feet would be so cold that you'd get up and go home after you'd sat there for two minutes! Nobody in their senses would sit out of doors on a day like this!'

They went on – and then, quite suddenly, they spied someone sitting on a log of wood not far off, busily drawing or painting on a sheet of paper set on a small easel.

'Look – *there's* someone painting!' said Valerie. 'Just when we'd been talking about it, too. How funny! Who is it? I can't see.'

'A man,' said Sam. 'A small man – rather thin. Oh, he's seen us. What's he doing – why is he looking scared?'

The man had got up hurriedly, snatched the picture and easel, picked up his stool, and was now running quickly through the trees. The children stared after him.

'Why did he go so suddenly? Was he scared of us?' wondered Sam. 'He was only painting a picture! Let's come and see if we can find out what bit of the scenery he was painting.'

They went to where they had seen the man. Valerie

shivered. 'It's very, very cold just here, isn't it?' she said. 'How *could* that man sit here as he did – without an overcoat on, too!'

'Look – what's this?' said Sam, and he bent down and picked up something. It was a sketchbook – quite small and very thick.

'He's left his sketchbook behind,' said Sam. 'What a pity!'

'What's in it?' asked Valerie. 'Let's look. Perhaps he's good at animals – or birds – or flowers.'

They opened the book – but to their disappointment, only the same things were drawn again and again. Beautiful pictures of ferns were on every page, their fronds showing even the smallest detail. How lovely – but how very much the same!

But at the end of the book was a page showing something different. At first the children couldn't imagine what the drawings were.

'They're like little patterns – all six-sided, and all small and very beautiful,' said Valerie. 'Now let me see – where did we hear something about six-sided patterns, Sam?'

'Oh, I know! Snow crystals!' said Sam. 'Don't you remember – our teacher caught some flakes of snow on a piece of black velvet for us – and gave us a magnifying glass – and when we looked through it, we saw that the snow was made of tiny crystals, all different – but every single one had six sides!'

'Yes! They were lovely – and these must be drawings of snow crystals!' said Valerie. 'The artist must be very clever. I wonder who he is. Is his name in the book?'

'No – but the pictures are signed with two initial letters,' said Sam. 'Look – just *J.F.*'

'*J.F.?* Now what would they stand for?' wondered Valerie. 'John something, I expect. How can we get his book back to him?'

'We can't,' said Sam. 'We'll just have to keep it carefully and hope we'll see him again – then we can give it to him.'

Now, that night, it was very, very frosty, and the two children pulled their blankets up close round their necks before they went to sleep. In the morning they awoke, and looked out of the window as usual to see what kind of a day it was. But they couldn't see through the windowpane! It was all frosted over.

'What's the matter with it?' said Sam, rubbing the pane hard – and then he stopped very suddenly. 'Valerie!' he called excitedly. 'Come and look here – tell me where you have seen something like this before!'

Valerie came to the frosted window. It was patterned and drawn with beautiful fern fronds – just like the drawings in the sketchbook they had found the day before!

'Oh – quick – let's compare these lovely designs with the ones in the book!' she said, and she fetched the book. Yes – the drawings were exactly the same as on the windowpane!

'It's the same artist!' said Valerie. 'It must be – and

now I know who he is! I know what those letters *J.F.* stand for!'

'What?' asked Sam.

'*Jack Frost*, of course!' said Valerie. 'And tonight, Sam, we are going to put his sketchbook out on this windowsill, so that if he comes again to draw on our window, he will see it, and take it!'

'Fine idea!' said Sam. 'I hope you are right, Valerie!'

'If the book is taken we shall *know* we are right,' said Valerie. 'Do let's watch for him, Sam.'

So that night they put the sketchbook on the windowsill, and then lay awake to watch for Jack Frost to come. But before long they were asleep and didn't awake till morning.

When they looked for the book, it was gone! And once again the windowpane was beautiful with all-over patterns of ferns. But this time something had been added in one corner.

Two letters had been drawn there – *J.F.* Yes – Jack Frost had signed his own picture on the windowpane, so that the children should know he had seen his book and taken it!

Has he ever signed his initials on *your* window? Watch out next time your pane is frosted over with a beautiful tracery of fern leaves – is *J.F.* down in the corner?

The Battle in the Toyshop

The Battle in the Toyshop

ONE CHRISTMAS time the toyshop in Windy Street was full of the finest toys in the land. There were great furry teddy bears, long-tailed donkeys, golden-haired dolls that could walk and talk, and marvellous soldiers on horseback. All these wonderful toys sat on the front shelves so that they could easily be seen, and behind them sat the cheaper toys.

The cheap toys were rather sad because they couldn't see who came into the shop to buy things; and of course, as you can guess, the most exciting times in a toy's life are when someone comes into the shop to buy something. Suppose that someone should buy them! All the toys hoped they would soon be bought and have a home of their own.

One night the cheap toys began to complain to the more expensive toys.

'Don't you think you could give us a little more room?' they asked.

'This big teddy bear is sitting down hard on my tail,' said a little clockwork mouse.

'And nobody can see us; we're quite hidden!' said a little brown dog, a pink cat and a blue rabbit.

'A good thing too!' said the biggest bear, rudely. 'Who wants to see common little things like you, when beautiful toys like us are here to be bought?'

'Some people can't afford to buy expensive toys like you,' said a cheap wooden Dutch doll. 'They want us for their children, and let me tell you this, you conceited bear – I have heard it said that many a child loves a little wooden doll like me better than all the furry bears or donkeys in the toyshop!'

'Pooh!' cried the biggest bear. 'I don't believe it!

Look at me, Dutch doll – I and my brother bears here are the finest toys in the shop!'

'Excuse me,' said the tallest golden-haired doll, in a little high voice. 'What nonsense you talk, Bear! We golden-haired dolls are easily the best toys here. We are the most expensive, anyhow.'

'You talk rubbish,' the bear said rudely. 'Why, only the girls like you dolls. Boys *and* girls like us bears. So just be quiet!'

All the dolls stood up in anger to hear the bear talk so rudely to them. The bear didn't care. He and his brothers made rude faces at the dolls.

'Now listen to us!' said all the marvellous toy soldiers together, for they only had one voice between them. 'Listen to us! We are the kings of this shop. We have swords and rifles, and we are the most powerful toys here. You dolls and bears don't know what you are talking about – best toys indeed! *We're* the best!'

Then the donkeys sat up straight and frowned very hard at the cheeky soldiers.

'You silly little things!' said the biggest donkey. 'Why, the whole lot of you would go into one of our boxes! You're all talking nonsense, bears, dolls, and soldiers. The donkeys are the best toys of all, and we are the kings of this shop, and the king of every playroom too!'

Well, dear me, you should have heard the dolls screaming, the bears shouting, and the soldiers clanking their swords when the donkey said that. How angry they all were! And then the Great Toyshop Battle began, a battle that is still talked of in every toyshop in the country.

The dolls rushed at the bears and began to smack them hard, and the bears doubled up their furry paws and began to punch the angry dolls. The soldiers drew their swords and marched on the donkeys, who at once kicked out and began to knock the soldiers down from the shelves to the floor.

Smack, smack! went the dolls.

Punch, punch! went the bears.

Clang, clang! went the soldiers.

Kick, kick! went the donkeys, and the soldiers tumbled one by one off the shelf, and went clattering down to the floor below, where they broke and lay still.

The cheap toys were frightened. They crept right to the back of the shelves and crouched there, quite still. They didn't want to join the fight. They were so afraid of being broken, and a broken toy is never sold, you know.

When the battle ended at last, what a dreadful sight was to be seen! All the dolls had their dresses torn, and three had cracks right across their pretty faces. The bears had bald patches all over them, where the dolls had pulled out handfuls of fur. All the soldiers were broken, except two that had fallen on the carpet – and every single donkey had its mane and tail slashed to ribbons by the swords of the fierce little soldiers.

When the toyshop woman came into her shop the

next morning to open up, what a dreadful shock she got! She stared all round and could hardly believe her eyes.

'What's happened in the night?' she said at last. 'Why, half a dozen cats from outside must have got in, and had a fight with all the toys. Oh dear, oh dear, what a dreadful thing! All the most expensive toys are spoilt! I shall have to send them to the jumble sale. I can't possibly sell them to my customers here!'

Just at that moment the door opened and in came a fat, jolly-looking man.

'Good morning,' he said. 'I'm holding a Christmas party today for twenty children, and I want lots of toys. Have you dolls, teddy bears, soldiers and donkeys?'

'I had,' said the toyshop woman, sadly. 'But look, something has happened in the night and they're all spoilt.'

'What a strange thing!' said the jolly man, in surprise. 'But never mind – I see you have lots of nice little toys quite unspoilt. I will take some of those.'

Then, to their great delight, the clockwork mouse, the pink cat, the blue rabbit, the brown dog, the wooden doll, the Jack-in-the-box, and many other cheap toys were taken down from the shelves and put on the counter for the man to see.

'Very nice, very nice indeed!' said the jolly man, picking up the pink cat and making it squeak by squeezing it in the middle. 'I shall be able to buy far more of these cheap toys than I could buy of the expensive ones, and I daresay the children will be better pleased to have four toys each instead of one!'

He bought eighty little toys and packed them carefully into the big case he had brought. Then he paid for the toys, said goodbye to the woman, and went off, delighted with all the toys he had bought. As for the toys, they were filled with joy too, to think they would soon have homes of their own with children to play with them.

The teddy bears, donkeys, dolls and soldiers were

all picked up and popped into a sack for the jumble sale. How sad they were!

'Why did we think such a lot of ourselves?' whispered a doll.

'We're being sent away like rubbish!' said a bear, almost crying with shame.

'Well, it's our punishment for being vain and foolish,' said the biggest donkey. 'We shall be sold for a few pennies each, and we're not worth any more now. We must just make up our minds to bear it, and be as nice as we can to the children who get us. But, oh, how silly we have been!'

And they certainly had been foolish, hadn't they?

Surprise on Christmas Morning

Surprise on Christmas Morning

'I'M GIVING SCAMPER a shilling bone from the butcher's for Christmas,' said Ben. 'Are you giving your budgie anything, Chris?'

'Yes. I'm going to buy a new little mirror to put in his cage, so that he can see himself,' said Christine. 'His other one got broken.'

'He'll like that,' said Ben. 'I wish we could give the little tame robin something for Christmas, too. He's so sweet the way he comes and looks in at the window each day, and taps on the glass when he's hungry.'

Mother laughed. She loved the robin too. 'Why don't you give *all* the birds something for Christmas?'

she said. 'You could do what my own family did when I was a child – buy a tiny Christmas tree, and hang it with things the birds like to eat!'

'Oh *yes*!' said Chris, pleased. 'Mother, we'll do that. I've got a little money over. How much would a tiny tree cost?'

'I'll buy the tree,' said her mother. 'You and Ben can dress it with things the birds like.'

'What things?' asked Ben. 'Bread, do you mean – and fat?'

'You can get biscuits, bore a neat hole through the middle and hang those on the tree,' said Mother. 'You can hang the tree with strips of bacon rind. You can buy peanuts and string them on thread for the tree – and you can get a coconut and break it in half, and then cut it up in little pieces to hang on the tree, too.'

'Oh Mother – you *have* got good ideas!' said Christine, pleased. 'We'll dress the birds' tree with all kinds of things – something for every single bird!'

Mother bought the little tree and the coconut and

the children bought a bag of peanuts and some sprays of millet, full of tiny seeds the birds loved. It was fun to dress the little tree with so many things.

Just as they were dressing it, Auntie Ruth came in to see Mother. 'How is your budgie, Christine?' she asked. 'Oh, there he is – can he talk yet?'

'Oh yes – he says his name, "Billy Budgie",' said Christine, 'and he says "Tom, Tom the piper's son" and "Hey diddle diddle." Does yours talk yet?'

Auntie Ruth looked sad. 'A dreadful thing happened yesterday,' she said. 'He escaped out of his cage when the window was open – and before we could shut it, he was gone! I really came round to ask you to keep a lookout for him.'

'Oh – we *will*!' said Christine. 'I *am* sorry, Auntie – he was so sweet, and so *lovely* in his green and blue! Oh dear – this isn't at all the right kind of weather for budgies to be out of doors – how will he find anything to eat?'

'I know – I keep thinking of that,' said Auntie

Ruth. 'Goodness me – why are you putting such queer things on that tree – bits of bacon rind – and what's this – a lump of suet!'

Ben laughed. 'It's a Christmas tree for the birds, Auntie,' he said. 'Especially for our dear little robin, who's as tame as can be. Look – there he is, peeping in at the window to see how the tree is getting on. I expect he has told all the birds about it already!'

Auntie thought it was a very good idea, and she helped them to tie on the biscuits and the millet sprays. The children had already threaded the peanuts on a long string, and had draped it over the tree from top to bottom. What a feast for the tits!

Auntie went off at last, having left some exciting-looking parcels for the two children. 'See you on Christmas Day,' she said. 'Granny and I will come in good time for midday dinner – and I hope you've got a nice big turkey!'

'We have!' called Ben.

'And don't forget to look out for my little lost

budgie,' said Auntie. 'I'm afraid he's going to have a very miserable Christmas!'

When the children had finished the tree they looked at it in delight. It really was splendid, and they had dressed it very generously with all kinds of things that the birds loved. Mother thought it was lovely.

'We'll put it out in the garden on Christmas Eve,' said Ben. 'That's tomorrow night – then when the birds wake up on Christmas morning, they'll see it in the garden and be *so* pleased!'

So when it was dark on Christmas Eve they carried out the little tree and put it carefully on their bird table, where the birds could easily see it. What a surprise for them!

Ben and Christine had such an exciting time opening their parcels on Christmas morning that they didn't even *think* of looking out of the window to see if the birds had found their own Christmas tree. It was only when Mother caught sight of a great many fluttering wings in the garden that she looked out and saw it in surprise.

'Ben – Christine – *look* at the tree you have given to the birds!' she said. 'Did you ever see such a crowd of birds round it – do look, it's wonderful!'

So it was. There were robins, sparrows, tits, chaffinches, starlings, thrushes, blackbirds – goodness me, the list was endless. How excited they were, and what a noise they made!

'It's as good as a pantomime!' said Ben, gazing out of the window. 'Chris – I've never seen so many birds together before! And look – there's even a greenfinch!'

'Ben – Ben, what's that bird just *behind* the tree?' said Chris. 'I can't quite make out – it's a brilliant colour – I do wish it would come round to the front – oh, here it comes – all blue and green and . . .'

'It's a BUDGIE!' shouted Ben, so excited that he made everyone jump.

'Ben – it's Auntie Ruth's budgie!' cried Christine, even more excited. 'It is, it is! Dear, dear little thing – it must have been hungry and seen all the other birds flocking to our tree – so it came too! Oh – can we possibly, possibly catch it?'

Mother was very excited too, now. She had a good idea. 'Christine – take Billy Budgie outside in his cage and put it down near the bird table. You know how he loves to chatter when he hears the other birds. He'll begin to talk and maybe Auntie's budgie will fly down to the cage – and you may be able to catch him!'

'Oh – splendid idea, Mother!' cried Ben, and Christine went at once to get her budgie's cage. To his surprise he was taken out into the garden and his cage was set down near the bird table. Then Christine went behind a bush and waited.

Billy Budgie was excited to see so many birds nearby and to hear them. He began to chatter and make all kinds of budgie noises, and he climbed up and down the cage wires.

The other little budgie heard him at once – and flew in delight to the cage. How the two budgies chattered to one another, and the second little bird tried its hardest to get into Billy Budgie's cage.

Christine stepped cautiously out from the bush. The birds on the Christmas tree flew away – all except the robin, who stopped to watch. The budgie stayed where it was, so interested in Billy Budgie that he didn't even notice Christine. She came nearer and nearer – and then a gentle hand came carefully down over the surprised little budgie clinging to the cage – and there he was, safely captured. In a trice Christine opened the cage door and popped him in with Billy Budgie!

Then, in triumph she carried the cage indoors, and at once all the wild birds flew back gladly to their little Christmas tree.

Before anyone could talk about the exciting capture, Auntie Ruth arrived with Granny, and everyone welcomed them joyfully.

'Happy Christmas! Happy Christmas!'

Presents and parcels were given out and for a time Ben and Christine forgot about the budgies. Then

Auntie Ruth came up to thank the children for their presents. She kissed and hugged them.

'Auntie – we've got *another* present for you!' said Ben, suddenly remembering the budgies. 'Come and look!' And he and Christine took her to the budgie's cage. Auntie Ruth gave one look, and then cried out in surprise.

'Oh! It's my budgie! My dear little lost budgie! Oh, Ben – oh, Christine – where *did* you find it? What a wonderful Christmas surprise! Budgie, hallo, hallo!'

'Hallo!' said her budgie and screeched excitedly.

'Budgie – say "Happy Christmas!"' said Auntie Ruth. 'Say "Happy Christmas, everybody!" just as I taught you to!'

'Happy Christmas, ebbody!' said the little blue and green budgie, and then he flew down beside Christine's budgie. 'Happy Christmas!' he said to him, and that made everybody laugh.

'Hey diddle-diddle!' said Billie, politely. 'Hey diddle-diddle!'

Wasn't it a good thing that Ben and Christine put out a Christmas tree for the birds? If they hadn't, the little lost budgie would have starved and died.

You simply never know what's going to happen, do you?

Rescuing Santa Claus

Rescuing Santa Claus

HAVE YOU ever heard the story of how Pitapat the gnome, Woffles the bunny and Muddle the monkey went to look for Santa Claus one Christmas time? If you haven't, I really must tell it to you.

Woffles and Muddle lived with Pitapat the gnome in One-Chimney Cottage. Woffles was a perfect pet of a bunny, with a nose that woffled up and down when he ate, so that was why they called him Woffles. The gnome was called Pitapat because he had very small feet that made a pitapat noise wherever he went. And Muddle the monkey was such a silly chap, and made so many muddles that you can quite easily guess how he got *his* name.

Now, it all began one morning in December. The three friends had just finished breakfast, and were sitting warming their toes at the fire. Just by Muddle the monkey was a calendar hanging on the wall. It was a tear-off calendar – you know the kind, don't you? Some calendars you have to tear off every day, some every week, and some every month. Well, this one was the sort you tear off every week, and Pitapat used to tear off a page every Monday. But he was too lazy to get up this Monday, so he called across the fire to Muddle.

'Hi, Muddle, stir yourself, and just tear off the calendar for me, will you?'

Muddle was very proud to do so. He thought it was a great treat to do anything like that. So he solemnly bent forward and tore the page right off, crumpled it up, and dropped it neatly into the wastepaper basket, as he had seen Pitapat often do.

Then he bent forward and stared at the calendar in

surprise. He rubbed his eyes, scratched his chin and stared at the calendar again. Then he borrowed Pitapat's spectacles and looked at the calendar through those, but it made no difference at all.

'*Well!*' said Muddle, 'who'd have thought it!'

'Thought *what*?' asked Pitapat. 'Give me back my spectacles, Muddle. You've put them into the wastepaper basket.'

'Why, today is Christmas Day, so the calendar says!' said Muddle. 'And Santa Claus hasn't been anywhere near us, or brought us any presents!'

'Christmas Day! It can't be!' cried Pitapat. 'Let me look at the calendar. And do give me my spectacles, Muddle. They're in the wastepaper basket, I tell you, so don't keep on looking in the coal scuttle. Oh, Woffles, *you* get them!'

So Woffles got Pitapat's spectacles for him, and Pitapat put them on and looked at the calendar. And he found that what Muddle said was quite right, for the calendar said:

December 25, Monday
CHRISTMAS DAY

'This is very extraordinary!' said Pitapat. 'Here is Christmas Day and no Santa Claus! He didn't fill our stockings or anything. Can it be that he has forgotten us, or is it that he is lost or something?'

'We'd better go and find out,' said Muddle. 'Come on, let's go and ask at the castle and see what has happened to him.'

For Pitapat and his friends were lucky enough to live in the same town as Santa Claus, and they often saw him standing at the door of his big castle on the hill above the town.

It didn't take them long to walk up the hill to the castle. Pitapat knocked at the door, and it was swung open by Big-Head, the porter.

'Good-morning, Big-Head,' said Pitapat, politely. 'Where is Santa Claus? Has he forgotten what date it is?'

'Not that I know of,' answered Big-Head. 'He

started out last week for old Witch Gruffles, as he heard she had some good conjuring tricks for sale, and he thought they might come in useful for Christmas presents. He hasn't come back yet.'

'Thank you,' said Pitapat, and Big-Head shut the door. The little gnome turned to his friends.

'That just proves it!' he said. 'I expect old Witch Gruffles has kept Santa Claus prisoner, and that's why he hasn't come back in time for Christmas.'

'Then we'd better go and rescue him,' said Muddle, firmly. 'We'll go and get our clockwork motor car, shall we, and drive off to Witch Gruffles this very minute.'

'It would be better to wait till night,' said Pitapat. 'Then we should find the witch asleep, perhaps. We don't want to be turned into green frogs or black beetles, do we? Don't look so frightened, Woffles. I won't let any harm come to you.'

Pitapat put his arm round the bunny, and all three went down the hill again. They went back to their cottage, and spent the day cleaning their clockwork motor car. At least, Muddle lost all the cleaning rags and polishes, Woffles found them again, and Pitapat used them.

Then, at nine o'clock, when it was very dark indeed, the three jumped into their car, and Pitapat took the wheel. Woffles cuddled up into Muddle's lap, and then *r-r-r-r-r-r-r*! The little red and white car was off and away over the dark road!

For three hours the little car went up hill and down, until at last it came to a thick wood. There was only a little path that led into the wood, so the car had to be left at the edge of the trees, whilst the three friends crept up the path. They soon came to a dark cottage, which they knew to be Witch Gruffles's!

'We'd better creep in through a window and see if Santa Claus is locked up anywhere,' whispered Pitapat. So they carefully opened a window, and then one by one dropped inside the cottage.

And, of course, Muddle immediately walked

straight into the dresser and knocked down quite a dozen plates!

In a moment the witch appeared at the door of the room they were in, and looked at them grimly by the light of her candle.

'What are you doing here?' she asked.

Now Pitapat didn't want the witch to know they had come to rescue Santa Claus, so he cast about in his mind for a good excuse.

'If you please,' he said, 'we came to see if you wanted anyone to help you in the house.'

'Oh, you did, did you?' said the witch. 'This is a funny time to call, I must say. But you can just stay here and work for me now you *are* here. You can sleep on the kitchen table.'

She went out again. Pitapat took Woffles in his arms and comforted him.

'Never mind,' he said. 'If we stay here one or two days we shall soon find out if Santa Claus is being kept a prisoner or not.'

So they stayed there for two days, and the witch kept them very hard at work. But not a sign did they see of Santa Claus, and at last they felt sure he wasn't there.

'Do you know where Santa Claus is, Witch Gruffles?' asked Pitapat at last.

'Yes, he went to visit the water pixies,' answered the witch, in surprise. 'He went there some days ago, I believe.'

Without a single word more, the three friends rushed out of the door and ran down the path to where they had left their car late on Monday night. Muddle wound it up, and then *r-r-r-r-r-r-r* it started off again.

'If only we'd asked the witch at first!' groaned Pitapat, 'we shouldn't have lost so much time. It's Wednesday now, and I expect the water pixies have been keeping poor old Santa a prisoner for ages!'

It was Friday by the time they came to the pond where the pixies lived and, of course, stupid Muddle drove the car straight into the pond!

'I forgot how to stop,' he said, 'and you see—'

'Oh, don't stop and explain now, you silly!' shouted Pitapat. 'I don't like sitting up to my neck in the water, if *you* do!'

They all got out, and looked at their poor car deep in the water. The pixies came swimming up, and looked too.

'We'll pull it out for you,' they said.

'Well, tell us, first of all, have you seen Santa Claus lately?' asked Pitapat, trying to wipe Woffles dry with his cap.

'Yes, he left us yesterday to go back to his castle,' said the pixies.

'Oh dear! Oh dear, oh dear!' groaned the gnome. 'And to think we've come all this way after him, thinking someone was keeping him prisoner.'

The pixies pulled and pushed at the car all that day and all the next, and at last they managed to get it out of the pond. Then Pitapat cleaned it up, and on Sunday morning it was ready for them to start back on their homeward journey again.

'Goodbye and thank you,' called the gnome, and *r-r-r-r-r-r-r*! Off went the car again.

It was late when they reached their cottage again – so late that the church clock was striking twelve as they slipped in through their front door and made their way to their little bedroom.

Then Pitapat suddenly stopped.

'There's a light in our bedroom,' he said. 'Whoever can it be?'

On tiptoe they went and peeped through the crack of the door. And then they saw a most extraordinary sight!

They saw Santa Claus hanging up clean stockings along their bedrail and filling them with all sorts of things!

At once the three friends rushed into the room and flung themselves on the jolly old man.

'Where have you been?' they cried. 'We thought you were a prisoner.'

'A Merry Christmas!' said Santa Claus, hugging them all.

'Why, Christmas was a week ago!' said Pitapat.

'Stuff and nonsense!' said Santa Claus. 'This is Christmas Eve!'

'But our calendar said *last* Monday was Christmas Day,' said Pitapat.

'You go and look again,' laughed Santa Claus, and, kissing Woffles on his nose, he shouldered his sack, jumped clean up the chimney and disappeared.

'Come down and look at the calendar again,' said Pitapat, puzzled.

So they all went downstairs and looked at it. Sure enough, it said exactly what they thought it would say – and then Pitapat suddenly had an idea! He looked in the wastepaper basket and took out the crumpled piece of paper that Muddle had torn off the calendar. And directly he looked he knew what had happened – and, of course, you've guessed!

Muddle had torn off two weeks instead of one. So

the next day *was* Christmas after all, and they hadn't missed it and Santa Claus hadn't forgotten it!

The Astonishing Christmas Tree

The Astonishing Christmas Tree

THE CHILDREN who lived at Apple Cottage, Little Street, had a tiny garden at the back of their house. It was so tiny that you couldn't really play any games in it at all, and so sunless that hardly any flowers grew there even in the summer.

But they had a tree in it – such a dear little tree. It was a fir tree, and the year before it had been the Christmas tree that the children up at the Big House had had for their party.

After the party the tree had been thrown away on the rubbish heap in the field outside the garden of the Big House. The children of Apple Cottage had found it there, forlorn and miserable, when they went to build a snowman in the field.

'I do believe it's the Christmas tree the Big House children had at their party,' said James, the eldest.

'I saw it through the window, when it was all dressed up with presents and pretties and candles,' said Jessie, the youngest. 'It had a lovely fairy doll at the top.'

'And now it's out here on the rubbish heap,' said Mary, one of the twins. 'All alone, with all its pretties taken off!'

'Couldn't we take it home and plant it?' asked Martha, the other twin. 'It's thrown away, so nobody would mind, would they?'

'Yes, let's!' said James. 'We can easily carry it between us. Then, if it grows all right, perhaps we might have it for a Christmas tree ourselves next year!'

'Look, there's one of the gardeners of the Big House!' said Jessie. 'Let's ask if we can have the tree.'

The gardener laughed, and said of course they could. So the children carried it home between them and planted it exactly in the middle of their tiny garden. Their mother smiled when she saw it, and made up her mind to save some money to buy presents to put on the tree the next Christmas time.

Now, as the children were planting the tree, something fell from the top branch. Jessie picked it up.

'Oh, look!' she cried. 'It's the wand that the fairy doll had. They must have taken her off the tree and left the wand by mistake!'

'Let's tie it to the topmost branch!' said Mary. 'There might be magic in it, and we might have good luck all the year!'

The others laughed at her, but James tied it carefully to the top branch, and there it stood, a funny little silver wand that shook whenever the branches shook.

'Let's all save our pennies through the year so that

we can buy lots of presents and candles to put on the tree next Christmas!' said James.

'Oh yes, do let's!' said Martha. 'It would be so lovely to have a proper Christmas tree of our own. Don't you think so, Mummy?'

'Yes, I do,' said Mummy. 'I was going to do exactly the same thing myself! Let's all have little boxes and put our pennies in till Christmas, and then buy all sorts of things to put on the tree!'

So everyone found a little box. James had an old chocolate box, and so had Jessie. Mary and Martha had custard powder boxes, and Mummy had a shoe box. And week by week pennies, halfpennies and farthings were dropped in. It was great fun. Mummy sometimes put a sixpence into her box, but not very often, for she was poor, and there were always many things to buy for the children. James was once given a shilling for stopping a runaway horse, and he put that in, too.

As Christmas time came near the children began to

get excited. Their boxes were quite heavy, and made a lovely jingling sound when they were shaken.

'Won't the tree look *lovely*!' said Jessie.

'We'll buy candles of all colours!' said Mary.

'And those pretty shiny ornaments,' said James.

'And lots of presents!' said Martha.

At last the day came when Mummy said they had all better open their boxes and go shopping. It was just two days before Christmas, so there was nice time to buy everything.

Very solemnly the children fetched their boxes, and sat down round the kitchen table.

'Open yours first, Jessie,' said Mummy.

Jessie opened her old chocolate box, and emptied a little pile of copper coins on the table. She counted them out. Eleven pennies, thirteen halfpennies, and six farthings.

'One and sevenpence!' she said, proudly.

'Now Mary and Martha,' said Mummy. They both had exactly the same – two shillings and twopence halfpenny each.

James had a lot, because of his silver shilling.

'Four shillings and sixpence halfpenny,' he said, proudly.

'And I've got eleven shillings and threepence!' said Mummy. 'What a lovely lot of things we can buy. Let me see, how much does that come to altogether?'

The children counted. 'One pound one shilling and ninepence halfpenny!' they said in delight.

Just at that very moment there came a knock at the door, and Mrs Brown, the next door neighbour, came in. She was crying, and looked terribly upset.

'What's the matter, Mrs Brown?' asked the children's mother.

'Oh, Mrs Jones!' wept Mrs Brown. 'Whatever shall I do! I've just had a telegram to say my little girl who's out in service at Bridgetown is very ill. I must go to her, I must.'

'Of course you must!' said everybody. 'Why haven't you gone?'

'I haven't got enough money to pay the price of the train ticket to Bridgetown!' sobbed Mrs Brown. 'My husband's out of work, and I've only two shillings. Could you possibly lend me a pound, Mrs Brown? I don't know when I can pay you back, but I'll try to, really I will!'

Mrs Jones fetched her purse.

'I've only enough to buy the children meals for the rest of the week,' she said, 'and I daren't touch the rent money.'

'Oh Mrs Jones, oh Mrs Jones!' wept Mrs Brown.

The children sat silent and looked at their money boxes in front of them. Then they looked at each other.

'Couldn't Mrs Brown have the money we've saved?' asked James, suddenly. 'We can easily do without it, as it's only for the Christmas tree.'

'Yes,' said Jessie, Martha, and Mary.

'You blessed little children!' said Mrs Brown, wiping her eyes. 'I never knew such dears as you, never!'

Well, before another minute was over, all the money that had been saved was emptied into Mrs Brown's purse.

'Don't let's talk about it,' said James. 'We couldn't do anything else, but we're all terribly disappointed, and talking will only make it worse.'

So not another word did the Jones family say about the money they had all saved up so carefully. But I don't know how many times they each stole to the window and looked sadly out on to the little tree.

Christmas Day came. Mummy had a plum pudding for them at dinner time, and everyone tried to be very gay and bright. But disappointment is disappointment, and the children couldn't help wishing that they were going to have a Christmas tree as they had planned.

At six o'clock, when it was very dark outside except for a few pale stars, Jessie ran into the back room just to see the little tree once more – 'in case it's lonely this Christmas!' she said to herself.

But what she saw astonished her so much that for

two whole minutes she stood and stared with her eyes and mouth as round as saucers. Then she found her tongue, and began to shout to the others.

'Mummy! James! Martha! Mary! Quick, quick! Come and look! Come and see the Christmas tree!'

The others came running in, and stared in the utmost astonishment just as Jessie had – for the little fir tree was transformed into a lovely Christmas tree! It was decked with gaily-burning candles and all sorts of shining ornaments. Exciting-looking presents hung about the tree, and crackers showed brightly here and there. It was the prettiest, most astonishing sight to see the little Christmas tree so gaily lighted up in the dark garden.

On the top of the tree was a little Santa Claus – and, strange to say, he carried the fairy's wand that James had tied to the tree! He seemed to smile and beckon to the children. Out they all went, helter-skelter, and danced round the tree in the greatest delight. It was far, far nicer than anything they could have done themselves, and the surprise was the best part of it all.

They soon had the presents off, and there were three for everybody. Mummy hadn't been forgotten, for she had a shawl and a new pair of shoes and a purse. As for the children, there were dolls and books, bricks and soldiers, sweets and chocolates.

But the most curious thing of all was what Mummy found in her new purse. She found exactly one pound one shilling and ninepence halfpenny, just what they all had saved. Don't you think that was funny?

And nobody to this day knows how it came about that the fir tree turned into a Christmas tree again. James says Santa Claus must have looked over the wall and seen them giving their money to Mrs Brown – and Jessie says *she* thinks the fairy's wand they tied to the tree had something to do with it!

A Christmas Story

A Christmas Story

SANTA CLAUS set out on Christmas Eve with his sack over his back – but do you know, it had a hole in it, which he didn't notice! He hadn't gone very far before a fine clockwork motor car fell out into the road, and after that a lovely fairy doll.

A clown was driving the motor car, and he was very much surprised to find himself in the road. The doll fell just by him, but except for making one of her wings the tiniest bit muddy she wasn't damaged at all.

'Hoy!' cried the clown. 'Jump into my car, and we'll soon catch up Santa Claus.'

The doll opened the door and climbed in. Then the

clown wound up his car, and off he started, bumping over the frosty road.

When he had gone a little way he saw two nuts and an orange, fallen out of the sack. The doll jumped out, picked them up, and stowed them in the back of the car. Then on they went again.

Soon they found an apple and a chocolate, and these went into the car too.

'Hoy-oy!' cried the clown, putting the brake on so suddenly that the fairy doll shot from the back seat into the front. 'Hoy-oy! There's a bright new penny and a banana, fairy doll! Put them in the car too!'

Well, very soon the car was packed with things that had fallen out of the hole in Santa's sack, and had been picked up by the fairy doll. It was quite easy to follow the way the old man went, because of all the dropped presents; but suddenly he discovered the hole, and pinned it up with a big safety pin. After that the clown didn't find any more presents on the road, and soon he was left far behind, quite lost.

'Hoy-oy!' he said to the fairy doll. 'We're lost! *Now* what shall we do!'

'Ooh!' said the doll. 'I don't like being lost, and I'm very cold.'

'Look, there's a little new house over there behind those trees,' said the clown. 'What about driving up and seeing if there are any children there? We were *meant* to be given to children, you know.'

So off he drove. He got the house cat to open the door for him, and then drove cleverly up the stairs to a room where two children were fast asleep. And would you believe it – Santa Claus had passed them by, and both their stockings were empty! Their house was a new one, and old Santa had somehow forgotten to add it to his list.

'Hoy-oy!' said the clown. 'This is where we come in useful! Unpack all that fruit and chocolate from the back of the car, fairy doll, and help me to stuff it into the stockings!'

In half an hour those stockings were full to bursting! Then, with the help of the fairy doll, the clown hoisted his car on the very top, and climbed into the driving seat. The doll sat herself on the other stocking, and there was peace.

The two children *were* pleased on Christmas morning! 'Three cheers for Santa Claus!' they cried. But they didn't hear a tired voice say – 'Hoy-oy! Three cheers for the clown and the fairy doll, you mean!'

Do-As-You're-Told!

Do-As-You're-Told!

THERE WAS once a little boy called Jimmy, who was really a little pickle! He simply would not do as he was told.

If he was told to walk on the pavement, not in the road, he would walk a few steps and then slip off into the gutter again. And his mother would say, 'Do as you're told, Jimmy.'

If his father said to him, 'Jimmy, sit up straight; don't loll like that,' he would sit up for half a minute and then loll forward again. And his father would say, 'Will you do as you're told?'

So all day long Jimmy heard the same thing: 'Do as

you're told.' But he never did. His friends called him 'Do-as-you're-told' because that is what they always heard when they were with Jimmy.

'Hello, here comes old Do-as-you're-told!' they would say. 'Come on, Do-as-you're-told. What shall we play today?'

And you may be sure that Do-as-you're-told would choose something he had been told not to do! Well, you can't go on like that for ever, and the day came when Jimmy got a shock.

It was a beautiful winter's day, but very, very cold. All the puddles in the road were thick ice. The duck pond was frozen too, and so was the village pond. The boys slid on the puddles, but they were not quite sure about the ponds. They ran to school, shouting and laughing that morning, sliding on the puddles and gathering the white frost from the top of the posts.

When it was time to go home from morning school, their teacher spoke to them.

'No sliding on the duck pond or the village pond yet,' he said. 'They are not safe. They may be safe tomorrow. Now, you hear me, all of you, don't you?'

'Yes, sir!' said the boys, and they trooped out into the frosty, sunny street, shouting and running.

'I say!' said Jimmy, as they came to the big village pond. 'Look at that shining ice! It's as safe as can be! Mr Brown is wrong.'

'No, you do as you're told, old Do-as-you're-told!' The boys laughed, pulling Jimmy away. But he shook himself free and gazed longingly at the frozen pond.

'Wouldn't I love a good slide over the ice!' he said. 'It feels so good! Whizzzzzz! And away we go, just as if we had wings on our feet. I think I'll try it and see if it's safe. I'm pretty sure it is.'

'Don't, Jimmy,' said the biggest boy. 'You know what Mr Brown said.'

'Well, it's too bad,' said Jimmy. 'I've been looking forward to sliding on this pond all the morning. And now he says we're not to! That means no sliding today

– and tomorrow the weather might be warmer and the ice will melt! We shall have missed our sliding!'

'Oh, come home!' said the boys. 'It's dinner time.'

But Jimmy wouldn't move. He simply longed to go sliding. Silly old Mr Brown to say the pond wasn't safe! Why, the ice was as thick as could be! Jimmy put his foot on it to try it. It didn't crack at all. He put his other foot on it, and stood with all his weight there. No cracks!

'It's safe, I tell you!' said Jimmy, in delight. 'Watch me slide!'

He set off over the frozen pond. He slid a lovely long way, and then, alas, he came to a thin piece! The ice cracked under his weight. It made a noise like the sound of a whip being cracked in the air.

'Oh! Oh!' cried Jimmy, in fright. He tried to stop himself sliding but he couldn't. He slid on and fell right into the water that came pouring through the cracks in the ice. He went down into the pond. It was icy cold – oh, so icy, icy cold!

Poor Jimmy! He tried to catch hold of the sides of the ice, but it was dreadfully slippery. He yelled for help. He was wet through, and the water was the coldest he had ever felt. Even his teeth began to shiver.

The watching boys were scared. The biggest one ran to the carpenter's shop nearby, shouting for a ladder. The carpenter picked one up and ran to the pond. He placed the ladder flat down on the ice and pushed it carefully towards Jimmy, who was still trying to catch hold of the edges of the ice. Nearer and nearer slid the ladder, and at last it reached Jimmy. He caught hold of the nearest rung, and then the carpenter pulled hard at the ladder. Jimmy was drawn right out of the water.

He began to clamber over the flat ladder, shivering and weeping.

The carpenter took him into his house, stripped off his wet clothes and dried him in front of a big fire. Jimmy was very frightened indeed. He couldn't stop shivering.

'Well, Do-as-you're-told, see what's happened to you!' said the carpenter, as he rubbed Jimmy dry. 'I suppose you thought you knew better than Mr Brown! Now you run home in this old suit of mine and tell your mother what's happened.'

Off ran Jimmy, looking very strange in the kind carpenter's big suit. When his mother heard what had happened she put him straight to bed, for she was afraid he would get a bad cold.

Two of the boys came to see Jimmy that afternoon, after school. 'What lessons did you do?' asked Jimmy, sitting up in bed.

'We didn't do any,' said Harry. 'Mr Brown took us up into the hills, where that old sheep pond is. It's much colder there than here and the sheep pond is frozen fast. We've been sliding all the afternoon! My goodness, Jimmy, we did have fun! You ought to have been there! The ice was as thick as could be!'

'We're going again tomorrow afternoon,' said George, the other boy. 'Perhaps you can come too, if you're all right, Jimmy.'

But Jimmy wasn't all right. He had caught a very bad cold and his mother kept him in bed for a week. And by the time he got up, the ice had gone! The weather had turned warm and not a single pond was frozen.

Jimmy was very unhappy. He had had a dreadful shock and caught a horrible cold – *and* missed all the fun of sliding up in the hills. He turned his face into his pillow and cried, for he felt rather small and miserable.

I shan't disobey again, he thought. *Nobody punished me for it – but I punished myself, and it was a dreadful punishment!*

Now nobody calls him Do-as-you're-told. He is just as much to be trusted as the other boys. I don't expect he'll be silly again, do you?

Something in His Stocking

Something in
His Stocking

'WAKE UP, SUE!' called Willie on Christmas morning. 'Do wake up! Let's look inside our stockings!'

'It's still dark,' said Sue, waking up suddenly. She switched on her light. 'Oh – *look* at our stockings! Full from top to toe. Quick, let's see what's in them. We'll take it turn and turn about to look. You first!'

'I've got a ship at the top of my stocking,' said Willie.

'I've got a baby doll!' said Sue. 'Look!'

It really was fun to empty their stockings right down to the toe – and even then there were more presents to see – presents that Daddy and Mummy had put at the ends of their beds. Willie had the last turn, because he could still feel something at the very bottom of his long, long stocking.

'What's this?' he wondered, scrabbling about. He pulled something out of his stocking – and stared in great surprise.

'Why – it's a *glove* – one big warm fur glove – not a new one, either!'

'How did it get there?' said Sue, surprised.

'I can't imagine,' said Willie puzzled – and then his eyes suddenly shone. 'Sue! Sue, you don't think it could belong to Father Christmas, do you? It's quite an *old* glove – and he could easily have stuffed it in with the toys, if he didn't notice what he was doing. He might have been in a hurry.'

'Yes – yes, I'm sure you're right!' said Sue. She felt suddenly excited. 'Oh, Willie – to think Father Christmas stood just over there last night – and stuffed his glove into your stocking in the dark!'

'What are we going to do with it?' said Willie.

'Shall we tell Mummy?'

'Not yet. Let's keep it a Christmas secret all to ourselves,' said Sue, who loved a secret almost more than anything. 'And Willie – when we go for our Christmas morning walk, let's take turns at wearing the glove! Fancy wearing a glove that belongs to Father Christmas! Do you suppose it's magic at all?'

'We can see,' said Willie. 'We'll wish a few wishes and things like that – just to see if they come true.'

'Put it in your drawer for now,' said Sue. 'I can hear Mummy and Daddy coming.'

It really was a most exciting secret to have. The children kept thinking of the glove all through breakfast. It added even more excitement to Christmas Day!

'Now go and get ready for your walk,' said Mummy, afterwards. 'Get a really big appetite for your Christmas dinner! Take this parcel to Granny for me and give her some Christmas hugs.'

The two set off, each wearing their own gloves. But

as soon as they were outside the house, they took it in turns to wear the big one belonging to Father Christmas. First Willie wore it, and he wished a wish. Just a little one to see if it would come true.

'I wish I could meet a kitten,' he said. 'A kitten coming along the road.'

But no kitten appeared. Then Sue had a turn and she wished for the snow to begin to fall. But it didn't. The sky remained clear and blue. After that they wished all kinds of things, but not one of them came true.

'The glove *isn't* magic,' said Willie. 'What a pity!'

'Look – there's Polly, with all her sisters and brothers,' said Sue. 'Let's stop and wish her a Merry Christmas.'

Polly was the daughter of the nice woman who came to help their mother clean the house. Her husband was dead, and she had eight children to bring up on her own. No wonder she often looked worried and ill!

'Hallo, Polly,' said Sue. 'Happy Christmas!'

'Thank you,' said Polly. 'But we shan't have anything but a miserable one. Mother went Christmas shopping last night with the money she'd saved up – but she slipped and fell and hurt her head – and while she was lying hurt on the road, somebody stole her purse. So we've got no Christmas dinner and no presents today.'

'Oh! No wonder you all look so miserable!' said Sue, unhappily. 'I'm sorry, Polly. I really am. Can't we do anything for you?'

'No,' said Polly, firmly. 'My mother says we're not to worry other people at Christmas time, so don't you go telling your mother or your granny anything. See? Mother would be cross if she knew I'd told you.'

'But just let me tell Mummy a *bit*,' begged Sue. Polly shook her head.

'No. It's bad enough having our own Christmas spoilt without upsetting other people's. We'll do all right. Don't you worry. We've got each other and

Mother feels better today.'

Polly said no more but went on her way, the other children, all smaller than she was, crowding after her. They hadn't said a single word all the time!

'They must have been too sad to say anything,' said Sue, unhappily. 'Willie, I'm going back home. I'm going to get some toys out of our cupboard, and the flowers off the playroom table, and my box of chocolates and my oranges and nuts. I want Polly's family to have them. We needn't say anything to Mummy, if Polly doesn't want us to – not till after Christmas, anyhow. But I simply *must* do something today.'

'So must I,' said Willie, and they hurried back. They put everything in a big paper bag and ran down to Polly's cottage. They put the bag on the doorstep ready to be found when the family returned home. They both felt better after that.

Next day, when they sat writing their thank you letters, which Mummy always said was a Boxing Day job, Willie looked at Sue.

'Sue – we ought to pack up Father Christmas's glove, and send it to him, with a letter,' he said. 'I'll write the letter – and I'm going to tell him about Polly and the others. Why didn't Father Christmas bring *them* things in their stockings?'

'Well, they haven't been in that cottage very long,' said Sue, 'I don't expect he even knew that any children were there. Old Mr and Mrs Harris lived there before.'

Willie wrote his letter. It was quite short and he wrote it as nicely as he could.

'Dear Father Christmas,

You left your glove in my stocking by mistake, so here it is. Thank you for all our lovely presents – but do you know that you forgot Polly Jones and all her seven brothers and sisters? They haven't a father and their mother is ill, and her purse was stolen on Christmas Eve. So they didn't have anything for Christmas. I do hope you will put them down on your list for next Christmas. Their address is Derry Cottage, Marks Crossley, Hants.

Love from Sue, my sister, and Willie.'

They put the letter and glove into a big envelope and went to post it. It only *just* slid into the mouth of the pillar box.

They forgot all about it after that, because treats and parties came along. But three days later Polly came running into the garden, her face crimson with happiness. She saw the children at the window and waved to them. They came out at once.

'Listen,' said Polly, 'something wonderful's happened!'

'What?' asked Sue and Willie together.

'Well, last night we heard the sound of bells, and then a knock came at the door,' said Polly. 'I went – and a funny little fellow was there – like an imp – and he had an enormous sack over his shoulder. Simply enormous!'

'Go on!' said Willie, excited.

'He put it down inside the door and said, "With apologies from Father Christmas for overlooking you – it won't happen again," and then, off he went at a run. And in another minute we heard the sound of bells again – and what do you think – when I looked up into the sky I could see somebody riding on a reindeer – just one reindeer, no sleigh. The little creature must have ridden on it all the way from Father Christmas's castle, carrying the sack!'

'Oh!' said Sue and Willie, so delighted that they went as red in the face as Polly was!

'And in the sack – well, we couldn't believe our eyes!' said Polly. 'A *big* turkey, sausages, a plum pudding, sweets and fruit, and goodness me, the *toys*!'

'How *lovely*!' said Sue. 'Enough for all of you?'

'More than enough!' said Polly. 'And a beautiful

warm coat for Mother – yes, he even remembered our mother! It's just too good to be true. But how in the world did Father Christmas know he'd forgotten us? Who *could* have told him?'

'We did!' said Willie, and told Polly about the glove, and how they had sent it back with a letter about Polly and her family. She listened in astonishment.

'But don't tell anyone about the glove, Polly,' said Willie. 'Please don't. Nobody would believe it, I'm sure. Oh, I do hope that Father Christmas will remember you all next year.'

I'm sure he will – and I hope he'll remember you, too. You'll know exactly what to do, won't you, if you find his glove left behind in your stocking!

Mr Pink-Whistle
and Santa Claus

Mr Pink-Whistle
and Santa Claus

ONE NIGHT, when Mr Pink-Whistle was snoozing in front of his fire, with a big cup of cocoa at his side, he thought he heard a strange little sound. He sat up straight and listened.

Then he called Sooty his cat. 'Sooty! Can you hear something – rather like a tinkling noise far away?'

Sooty popped his black head round the door. 'Yes, Master – I've heard it for some time. It comes from the sky.'

'Nonsense, Sooty!' said Pink-Whistle, taking a sip of his cocoa. 'Surely you don't think the stars are suddenly tinkling as well as twinkling?'

Sooty laughed. 'No, I don't,' he said. 'But it's true, Master – the sound is coming down from the sky. It's almost as if there's a tiny plane up there, going round and about looking for a landing place, and tinkling all the time.'

'Planes don't tinkle,' said Pink-Whistle. 'It can't be a plane! Listen – it sounds as if it's coming nearer! Let's go outside and look.'

So out they went into the cold, frosty night, for it was December, and only two days before Christmas. They stood looking up into the starry sky, listening for the tinkling.

'There – I heard it again,' said Sooty. 'And look, Master – what's that circling round up there? It's not a plane. Whatever can it be?'

The two stared hard into the sky. They saw a small object very high up, circling round and round. It came lower and lower – and suddenly Sooty gave a loud mew of excitement.

'Master! It's a tiny sleigh, very tiny – with one

small reindeer pulling it!'

'Then it must be Santa Claus coming to pay me a visit!' Pink-Whistle said in excitement.

'No. It's not Santa Claus. It's someone small,' said Sooty, who had wonderful eyesight. 'Santa Claus is big and round and jolly. Look – the little sleigh is coming lower and lower.'

'Get the lamp from my room and put it out here in the garden,' said Pink-Whistle, excited. 'Quick, Sooty!'

Soon the lamp was shining brightly in the middle of the lawn. Sooty and Pink-Whistle were glad to see that the reindeer seemed to be coming straight down to it, pulling the tiny sleigh behind him.

'Here he is! Careful, reindeer, don't knock the lamp over!' shouted Sooty. 'That's right. Stand still now – you're safe.'

The sleigh was indeed small – and in it sat a perky little fellow in a red tunic, cloak and feathered hat. He leapt out of the sleigh and bowed to Pink-Whistle.

'I hope I am speaking to the famous and good-hearted Mr Pink-Whistle,' he said. 'I have had quite a time trying to find your house. I come with a message from Santa Claus.'

'Well, well, well!' said Pink-Whistle, most amazed. 'How extraordinary. Please come in and have some hot cocoa.'

Sooty led the way and the three of them went indoors, leaving the reindeer on the lawn trying to munch the frosty grass. Sooty fetched an old coat and threw it over him to keep him warm.

Pink-Whistle made the messenger sit down in front of the fire. He was a merry-looking fellow, and Pink-Whistle liked him. 'Now,' he said, 'what's your message? If I can do anything for that good fellow, Santa Claus, I will. Does he want a list of children's names – children who really do deserve a lot of presents?'

'Well, no, he doesn't,' said the little fellow, drinking his cocoa. 'I say, isn't this good? We never have cocoa like this in Santa Claus's castle. That cat of yours certainly knows how to make it!'

'Me-ow-ee-OW, I do know how!' said Sooty, proudly.

'Gracious – he can speak in rhyme too!' said the little fellow. 'By the way, my name is Joll – short for Jolly, you know.'

'It suits you,' said Pink-Whistle, 'but do tell me why you've come.'

'Well, it's like this,' said Joll. 'Santa Claus is in bed with a shocking cold and cough. Good gracious, when he coughs, the whole castle shakes!'

'Goodness me – I hope he has a clever doctor,' Pink-Whistle said in alarm.

'Yes, he has – so good that he won't let Santa Claus get up till next week,' said Joll.

'Ah – that's very sensible,' said Pink-Whistle. 'He'll soon get better if he's kept in bed.'

'Yes – but it's very, very awkward,' said Joll. 'Have you forgotten that Christmas is in two days' time –

and that tomorrow night Santa Claus has to drive his sleigh and take a sack of toys to put in children's stockings? Well, how can he do that if he's in bed?'

'Oh dear – no, he can't, of course,' said Pink-Whistle. 'My word – whatever's to be done?'

'Aha! That's where you come in!' said Joll. 'Mr Pink-Whistle, Santa Claus wants to know if you'll take his place in his sleigh on Christmas Eve? It has to be someone the children love, you see, someone they won't be scared of if they happen to see him – someone who really loves children. Well now – what about it?'

'What? Me? Me in Santa Claus's sleigh – me climbing down chimneys!' said Pink-Whistle, in amazement. 'I couldn't. I don't know how to. I'd get stuck.'

'No, you wouldn't,' said Joll. 'Didn't you know that Santa Claus always sprays himself with some special magic oil, so that he can slip down any chimney, no matter how small?'

'No. No, I certainly didn't know that,' said

Pink-Whistle, really astonished. 'But still – no, I really don't think I could drive a sleigh through the sky. I might fall out.'

'I could strap you in, and come with you,' said Joll. 'Please do this for Santa Claus. The only other person whom we could ask would be Big-Ears, little Noddy's friend, but we really think that you would be better, because you know the children better than Big-Ears does. He lives in Toyland and knows toys better than children.'

'All right. I'll do it,' said Pink-Whistle, beginning to feel excited. 'Yes – I'll do it!'

'Right!' said Joll, pleased. 'I'll get straight back and tell Santa Claus. He'll be delighted. I'll come here on Christmas Eve and show you how to drive the reindeer. There will be four of them. And I'll help you with the toys too, and bring the list of children.'

'My word – whoever would have thought I'd take Santa Claus's place one Christmas Eve!' said Pink-Whistle, wondering if he was in a dream. 'It's a great honour, Joll, a very great honour. Please tell Santa Claus I hope he'll soon be better and that I'll do my best.'

'Can I come too?' asked Sooty, who had been listening in great excitement. But nobody answered him. Pink-Whistle was showing Joll out of the door, and thanking him for coming.

He watched Joll jump into the sleigh and shake the reins – and then up into the sky they went, the bells jingling merrily.

'Isn't it exciting, Sooty?' said Pink-Whistle, coming indoors, all smiles.

'You'll have to wear a very thick coat, Master,' said Sooty. 'It will be very, very cold driving in a sleigh up in the wintry sky.'

'I haven't got a very thick coat,' said Pink-Whistle. 'But never mind. I'll feel so excited that I shan't notice the cold. I'm sorry you can't come, Sooty. There wouldn't be room for you in the sleigh. My word – what an adventure I'm going to have!'

On Christmas Eve, Sooty's sharp ears once more heard the sound of bells far away in the sky. He ran to the window. 'Quick! Joll's coming!' he said. 'Get ready, Master. See – down comes the big sleigh – with four fine reindeer tossing their antlers!'

There came a knock at the door, and there stood Joll, beaming all over his face. He carried a red cloak and hood over his arm.

'Ready?' he said. 'I've brought you Santa Claus's cloak to wear – it's so bitterly cold up in the sky tonight. And here's the list of children.'

'Oh – I don't want to wear a cloak and hood,' said Pink-Whistle. 'Children might think I'm Santa Claus, and I'm not. I don't even have a beard!'

'Master, you must wear the warm cloak,' said Sooty, 'and take a hot-water bottle for your feet. I don't want to have you in bed with a cough and cold for weeks!'

'All right, all right,' said Pink-Whistle, in a grumbly voice. 'I'll wear the cloak – but I won't wear the hood, I shall wear my own hat – and I certainly shan't take a hot-water bottle for my feet.'

'Come along, quickly, or we'll be late,' said Joll, and he put the red cloak round Pink-Whistle's shoulders. 'Keep your hat on if you want to – but hold on to it when the wind blows!'

Jingle-jingle-jingle – the sleigh rose into the air pulled by the four excited reindeer. Joll drove them for some way, then handed the reins to Pink-Whistle, who found that he could drive four lively reindeer quite easily. My word – how the wind streaked past his nose, and how glad he was that his hat was jammed on his head so tightly. He was cold even in the thick red cloak – and as for his feet, they were like ice!

'I wish I had brought a hot-water bottle for them, after all,' he said. And even as he said that he felt a slow, cosy warmth settling on his feet. *Magic!* he thought. *I wished for a hot-water bottle and it came! Well, well, I am enjoying this!*

It was most exciting to land gently on rooftops,

beside tall chimneys, and even more exciting to find how easy it was to slip down them, once Joll had sprayed him with the magic oil! Pink-Whistle slid down each chimney as easily as a snake, and landed in bedroom after bedroom, where sleeping children lay dreaming of the presents they would find next morning.

It's nice to fill stockings, thought Pink-Whistle. *I'll put an engine into this stocking – and a doll into that – and where's that little car? Here it is. And there's a book as well. Dear me, how excited these sleeping children will be tomorrow morning.*

I can't tell you how many stockings Pink-Whistle filled that Christmas Eve, nor how many sleeping children he saw. All but one were sound asleep – one small boy woke up as Pink-Whistle landed on the hearth rug in his bedroom. How he stared when he saw someone he thought was Santa Claus – wearing a top hat!

'You're not Santa Claus,' he said. 'Where's your

beard? And why haven't you a hood instead of a hat? I'll shout and call my mother!'

Well, Pink-Whistle disappeared up that chimney at lightning speed! Good gracious! He didn't want to face an angry mother! When he sat panting on the roof he remembered that he hadn't had time to fill the boy's stocking. So he carefully dropped a few toys down the chimney, hoping they would land safely on the hearth rug. Then he scrambled into the sleigh beside Joll, and away he went.

'Well, I did enjoy that!' he said, when it was all over, and he was safely driving home in the sleigh, his feet being warmed again by what felt like a nice warm and furry hot-water bottle. 'Please thank Santa Claus for giving me the chance of visiting the children on Christmas Eve, Joll. It was wonderful! Oh – here we are on my lawn again. Like a nice hot drink?'

'No thanks,' said Joll. 'I must go and report to Santa Claus. He'll be longing to know if everything went off all right.'

'Well – I'll go and report to Sooty, my cat, too,' said Pink-Whistle, getting out of the sleigh, and going to pat the reindeer, and give them a lump of sugar each.

'Oh – Sooty knows all about your exciting evening,' said Joll, with a chuckle. 'He stowed himself away under the rug; didn't you know? He was your hot-water bottle, Mr Pink-Whistle, and curled himself up on your feet to keep them warm! Come out, Sooty, you rascal!'

And out leapt Sooty, and rubbed himself against Pink-Whistle. 'I enjoyed it all too!' he said. 'Now let's go in and have a hot drink, Master, and talk about our wonderful evening!'

They stood and waved goodbye to Joll and the fine reindeer. The bells sounded more and more faintly, and then died away.

'You're a naughty cat, Sooty,' said Pink-Whistle, when they were sitting drinking hot lemon by the warm fire. 'But I must say you were a very good hot-water bottle! Listen – one little boy was awake and saw me. I'm afraid he'll never believe in Santa Claus again, because he saw my top hat.'

'Well, he'll believe in *you* all right!' said Sooty. 'Let's have this exciting evening put into a story, Master – and then when the boy reads it, he'll know that he was the only child in the world who saw you instead of Santa Claus this Christmas Eve! How surprised he must have been to see someone coming down the chimney in a top hat!'

I must say I'd have been surprised too – but I'd have known it was kind old Pink-Whistle, wouldn't you?

On Christmas
Night

On Christmas Night

'NOW YOU twins must go to sleep quickly or Santa Claus won't come and fill your stockings,' said Mother, on Christmas Eve.

The twins talked after she had gone. 'I always try to stay awake, but I never can,' said Dan. 'I wish we could wake up when Santa Claus comes upstairs.'

'I know what we'll do!' said Daisy. 'We'll put a box by the door, so that he'll step into it and fall when he comes in the room! Then we shall hear him.'

'Yes. And we'll pile a whole heap of books nearby too, so that he'll knock those down and make an awful noise!' said Dan.

'And we'll wind string all about the place so that he'll get caught!' said Daisy. 'Then we really shall hear him and see him.'

So they put out an empty box by the door, and built up an enormous pile of books nearby. Then Dan wound string here, there and everywhere! What a trap for poor Santa Claus!

The twins fell asleep. In the middle of the night they awoke with a jump. *Crash!* The pile of books had fallen over. Someone had trodden in the box and tripped into the books. And by the visitor's angry grunts it sounded as if he had been well caught by the string!

Neither of the twins dared to get out of bed and put on the light. They lay trembling in the darkness. Would Santa Claus be very cross with them?

Then they heard their father's voice, speaking in a low tone to their mother, who had come to see what had caused all the noise.

'These tiresome twins! They've put a box by the

door and I trod in it and upset a pile of books or something and now I'm all caught up with string. I tell you, these children won't have a single thing in their stockings if this is the way they behave!'

Father and Mother went away. Dan and Daisy slipped out of bed, cleared up the mess, and took down the string. Then they hopped back to bed, glad that they had only caught Daddy, and not Santa Claus after all.

'Perhaps he will fill our stockings,' whispered Daisy. He did – but they didn't deserve it, did they?

The Great Big Snowman

The Great Big Snowman

JANE AND JOHN ran out into the snow. It lay thick on the ground and was so white that it was quite dazzling in the sunshine.

'Let's build a snowman!' cried Jane. 'We have plenty of time, John. We can make a really big one!'

So they set to work. First they made a big snowball, and then they rolled this all the way down the garden and back. It got bigger and bigger as it rolled along, and when it was big enough the children used it for the snowman's body, building it up higher once they had got it into place.

He was very tall – as tall as the children – and when

he had his big, round snow head on, he was just a bit taller. Really, he was a very grand snowman indeed.

'Daddy! Daddy! Will you lend us an old hat to put on the snowman's head?' called the children, when Daddy looked out of the window.

'I say! What a fine snowman!' said Daddy, in surprise. 'Yes, you can have a hat for him. I'll bring you my old garden hat. It has a hole in it now, so I shan't use it any more. The snowman is welcome to it!'

Daddy brought out the hat, and also an old pair of gardening gloves for the snowman's cold hands. He found some large, round stones too, and these the children put all the way down the snowman's body for buttons. He did look grand.

'Mother! Come and look!' shouted the children. So Mother came, and she thought the snowman looked really fine. She gave Jane and John a scarf to put round his neck. It was bright red, so you can guess how grand he looked. The children were delighted with him!

When they went to bed that night, they looked out of the window at him. There was only a very little moon, so they could not see him very well; he looked like a man standing in the middle of the garden.

'Doesn't he look real now?' said Jane to John. 'Suppose he came alive! Wouldn't it be fun?'

'Snowmen never come alive. Don't be silly, Jane,' said John. The two children hopped into bed and soon fell asleep. Jane dreamt she had gone to a party with a hundred snowmen, and John dreamt he had been turned into a snowman himself and couldn't walk or run.

Now all this time the snowman stood alone in the garden. And, in the middle of the night, two other people came to the garden. They were two burglars, and they had come to steal the silver cups and dishes that the children's father had won playing golf. They crept up the garden path, but suddenly they stopped.

'I say, Bill!' whispered one. 'There's someone in the garden tonight. Look!'

Bill looked to where his friend pointed, and he saw the old snowman, standing quite still in the middle of the lawn. The snowman looked real – like a big man watching them. The two men were frightened.

'Is it the policeman, Jim?' whispered Bill.

'It looks like him,' said Bill. 'Let's hide here till he goes off.'

So the two men hid by the hedge, and kept as still as could be. They watched the snowman, and wondered why the policeman, as they thought, didn't move.

'He *must* be watching for us!' said Bill. 'Let's creep off, Jim. We may be able to get away before he sees us.'

So the two men began to creep down the path. And just at that moment, who should come down the road but the *real* policeman, riding quietly on his bicycle.

The men were so busy watching the snowman that they didn't see or hear the policeman at all. They were creeping out of the front gate when the policeman saw them, and, quick as lightning, he jumped off his bicycle, flashed his light into their faces, and recognised them.

'Oho, Bill and Jim!' he said. 'And what may you be doing here, I'd like to know?'

He blew his whistle loudly, and round the corner came another policeman on a bicycle, and the children's father also came running out. The men were caught, and the policeman told them they must go to the police station with him.

'We weren't doing anything,' said Bill sulkily. 'And anyway, there was a policeman watching us from the grass over there. *He'll* tell you we didn't go into the house or do anything we shouldn't. Talk about policemen! This road seems full of them tonight!'

'A policeman on our grass!' said Daddy, in astonishment. 'Whatever do you mean?'

'Well, who's that over there, then?' said Bill, and he pointed to the snowy lawn.

The policemen flashed their lamps over the grass,

and there stood the old snowman, in Daddy's hat and Mummy's scarf.

'Stars and moon, it's only a snowman!' said the two burglars, in disgust. 'To think we were scared by that! Why, we thought it was a policeman!'

Daddy laughed. 'The children will be pleased to hear that their snowman saved us from being robbed tonight!' he said.

'Yes sir,' said the two policemen, grinning. 'Come on now, you two men. We want you for many robberies, and we're glad to get you. We're grateful to the snowman for helping us to catch you!'

Off they went – and Daddy went to bed. In the morning he told the children all that had happened, and you can guess how excited they were.

'Fancy our snowman saving us from robbers,' cried John. 'Oh, Jane, let's go and say thank you to him!'

So out they went, but, you know, it was a warm morning and the sun had been out for some time, so there was nothing much left of the snowman except a little heap of snow, Daddy's hat and gloves, and Mummy's scarf.

'Well, you were a fine snowman while you lasted!' said John. 'Thanks so much for all you did!'

The snowman didn't answer a word, but I expect he was pleased, all the same.

Peter's Christmas
Surprise

Peter's Christmas Surprise

PETER WAS the most unhappy boy you could possibly imagine – and I don't wonder, because he had got measles just at Christmas time! Did you ever know such bad luck?

'No parties, no pantomimes, no Christmas tree!' he groaned. 'Nothing can make up for such bad luck!'

'Don't be so miserable,' said his mother. 'If you face trouble in the right way something always turns up to make things better.'

Peter was just going to say that he couldn't possibly be more miserable when he saw that his mother was just as upset as he was. She loved him and she couldn't bear to think he would be missing everything. So Peter pretended he didn't care, after all, and made himself smile at his mother. But he knew inside himself that nothing could make him feel happy that Christmas time.

On Christmas Eve his mother made him comfortable in his bed and said good night to him. It was a bitterly cold night, and he had a cheerful fire blazing. Peter lay watching the flames for a little while, and then he fell asleep.

He woke up just as the clock downstairs was striking one on Christmas morning – and he heard a very curious sound. Just like someone snoring! Peter sat up and looked about. Whatever could it be? There was still a nice little fire on the hearth, and Peter could see dimly round his room – and goodness, gracious me, there was someone sitting in the armchair by the fire, *fast asleep*!

Peter thought it must be his daddy, so he got out of bed to wake him – but it wasn't. It was someone big and fat, someone with a long white beard, someone in a red cloak and hood! Yes, you've guessed right – it was Santa Claus!

Peter gave a cry of astonishment – and Santa Claus woke up. He rubbed his eyes and looked all round. 'Bless us all!' he said, jumping to his feet. 'I've been asleep! Whatever is the time?'

'Just past one o'clock!' said Peter, feeling most excited. 'I say, sir, how did you get here?'

'Down the spare room chimney,' said the jolly old man. 'I crept in here to fill your stocking, and when I saw your nice fire I sat down to warm my hands. It's bitter outside, you know, and I get frozen holding my reindeer reins. I suppose I must have fallen asleep! If you hadn't wakened me I should have been here till morning, and *then* what would all the children have done! Aren't you lucky to have a fire like this!'

'It's only because I've got measles,' said Peter. 'I hope you won't catch it from me.'

'Of course I shan't,' said Santa Claus. 'Well, look

here, I must be off. You'll have to see me filling your stocking, but don't say anything about it, will you?'

He filled Peter's stocking from toe to top, then shook hands and slipped out of the room. Peter fell asleep again, thinking that he must be the only child who had ever seen Santa Claus filling his stocking. And the last thing he thought was – *Well, what a good thing I had measles! If I hadn't, I shouldn't have had a fire in my bedroom and Santa Claus wouldn't have warmed his hands, and, and* . . .

But by that time he was fast asleep!

Bunny's First
Christmas

Bunny's First Christmas

'IT'S CHRISTMAS time!' said the big rocking horse in the toyshop, one night when the shop was shut, and only the light of the streetlamp outside lit up the toys sitting on the shelves and counters.

'What's Christmas?' asked a small bear who had only just arrived.

'Oh, it's a lovely time for children,' said the horse, rocking gently to and fro. 'They have presents, you know, and Father Christmas comes on Christmas night and fills their stockings with all kinds of toys.'

'You'll never go into a stocking, Rocking horse!' said a cheeky monkey.

'No, I shall stand in somebody's playroom and give them rides,' said the horse. 'I shall look forward to that. I've been here a long time – too long. But I'm very expensive, you know, and people often haven't enough money to buy me.'

'I should like to live with children who would love me and play with me,' said a fat teddy bear. 'I shall growl for them – listen – *Urrr-rrrr*!'

'Don't!' said the little furry rabbit. 'That frightens me. I think you're going to bite me.'

'You know he wouldn't,' said the clockwork sailor, leaning down from the shelf above. 'Come on, Bunny, let's have a game.'

The rabbit jumped down to the floor at once, and the clockwork sailor landed near him. He loved the sailor, who wouldn't let any of the bigger toys tease him or frighten him. Sometimes the pink cat chased him and the little rabbit couldn't bear that!

'Sailor,' said the rabbit, when all the toys were playing together. 'Sailor, we're friends, aren't we?

Sailor, you won't leave me if you are sold and go to live with some children, will you?'

'Well – I shan't be able to help it,' said Sailor. 'You're my very best friend and I'm yours, and I hope and hope we'll be sold together – but you never know!'

The rabbit worried about that, and next day when customers came in and out of the shop, buying this toy and that, the little rabbit hoped that he and the clockwork sailor would be bought by the same person.

But they weren't! An old woman came in and asked for a sailor doll for her granddaughter whose father was a sailor – and the shop lady at once took down the clockwork sailor from his shelf.

'He's fine,' said the little old woman. 'Yes, I'll have him. My granddaughter Katy will love him! Will you wrap him up for me, please?'

'Goodbye, Sailor!' whispered the little rabbit, sadly. 'Oh, I shall miss you so! Goodbye, and be happy!'

Sailor only had time to wave quickly while no one was looking. Then he was wrapped up in brown paper and carried out of the shop, leaving Bunny all by himself. Poor Bunny! He felt lonely and unhappy without his friend by his side. He hoped that the bear wouldn't growl at him or the pink cat chase him.

But that very day he was sold too! A big, smiling woman came in and bought a great many toys at once.

'They're for a Christmas tree,' she said. 'I am giving a party on Boxing Day for my little girl and her friends, and we've got a perfectly lovely tree to decorate.'

'You'll want a pretty fairy doll for the top, then,' said the shop lady, pleased. 'And what about a little teddy bear and a doll or two?'

'Yes. And I'll have that toy ship – and that wooden engine – and that Jack-in-the-box,' said the customer. 'And I really must have that little rabbit – he's sweet!'

Bunny was sold! He couldn't believe it. He was sold at last and would leave the toyshop he knew so well.

Bunny was very pleased to be going with so many

other toys he knew. But, oh dear, each of the toys would be given to a different child at the party, so he wouldn't have any friends at all after Boxing Day!

The other toys were terribly excited. It was fun to be sold and leave the toyshop. It would be splendid to be part of the decorations on a beautiful Christmas tree and have crowds of children admiring them. And it would be simply lovely if they were lucky enough to be given to a kind and loving child who would look after and play with them and perhaps even cuddle them in bed.

When they arrived at the smiling lady's house, Bunny was surprised to see such a big Christmas tree. It almost reached the ceiling!

'I don't think I want to be hung up there,' he said to the fat teddy bear, who had been sold for the tree too. 'I might fall off and hurt myself.'

'Don't be such a coward,' said the bear. 'Ah – here comes someone to see to us! Cheer up, you silly little rabbit, and remember, if you are given to some horrible child, you must just run away and find a new home!'

'Run away? How?' asked the rabbit, anxiously. But the bear was very busy growling at that moment, because someone was pressing him in the middle where his growl was kept!

'*Urrrr*!' he said proudly. '*Urrrr*!'

The little rabbit was hung high up on the tree, where he dangled to and fro. He didn't like it. The ground seemed so far away! All the other toys hung there too, and pretty fairy lights shone brightly in red, blue, yellow and green from the top of the tree to the bottom.

'The party's tonight!' said a rag doll next to him. 'Not long to wait now! Doesn't the fairy look wonderful at the top of the tree?'

Soon the rabbit heard the sound of children's voices and laughter. They were playing games in another room. Then someone came into the big room where the tree stood and switched on all the fairy lights again. The tree glowed and shone, and all the pretty ornaments on it glittered brightly. The toys looked lovely as they hung there.

How the children cheered and clapped when they came running in and saw the lovely tree.

'It's beautiful!' they shouted. 'Oh, look at the toys! Can you see the fairy doll? Wave your wand, Fairy Doll, and do some magic!'

'Now, there is a toy for everyone,' said the smiling lady who was giving the party. 'Harry, here is a ship for you,' and she gave him the toy ship. 'Lucy, here is a lovely rag doll. I know you want one. Molly, I have just the toy for you – a bear with a growl in his tummy.'

Soon there were only a few toys left on the tree. The little rabbit looked down on the children. Was there a little girl called Katy there? The sailor doll had been bought for a Katy. Oh, wouldn't it be wonderful if he was given to her, the same little girl who had the clockwork sailor?

Who was Bunny going to? He looked and looked at the children. He did hope that he would be given to somebody kind – a nice little girl, perhaps, with a merry face.

'And now, what about a present for you, Peter,' said the kind lady. 'You're not very old – I think you shall have this little furry bunny. Here you are!' So Bunny went to Peter, who held him very tight indeed, and squeezed him to see if he had a squeak inside. But he hadn't.

Bunny didn't like Peter very much, especially when he dropped him on the floor and somebody nearly trod on him.

'Be careful of your little rabbit, Peter,' said a big girl.

'I don't like him,' said Peter. 'I wanted that wooden engine.'

Poor little rabbit! He wondered if he could run away, just as the teddy had suggested. He didn't want to go home with Peter. He was sure he was one of the horrible children he had heard spoken about in the toyshop. But he did go home with Peter, and with him went a jigsaw puzzle for Peter's sister.

'Give this to your sister, Peter,' said the kind lady. 'It is such a pity she's in bed with a cold and can't come. This jigsaw shall be her present.'

Peter carried the rabbit and the jigsaw home. As soon as he got there he went up to his sister's bedroom.

She was in bed, with a large hanky under her pillow.

'Look – they sent you a jigsaw from the party,' said Peter. 'And all I got was this silly little rabbit!'

'Oh, Peter – he's sweet!' said the little girl in bed. 'I've so many jigsaws – why don't you take this one and I'll have the bunny instead. He shall come into bed with me. He looks rather lonely and, after all, he's only a baby!'

'All right. I'd much rather have the jigsaw,' said Peter. And he threw the rabbit to his sister and went out with the jigsaw underneath his arm.

Bunny landed with a thud on the bed, feeling very sorry for himself. Nothing seemed to be turning out as he had hoped.

The little girl picked him up gently and looked at him.

'Yes, I like you,' she said, giving him a hug. 'You shall sleep with me at night, so long as you don't mind sharing my bed with another toy. Look, here he is – my very best new toy!'

She pulled back the sheet – and Bunny stared in amazement. He couldn't believe his eyes. Who do you suppose was cuddled down in the bed, looking very happy? Why, it was Sailor!

Yes, it was the clockwork sailor doll, the one from the toyshop, Bunny's own special friend. Sailor almost sat up in surprise, but just in time he remembered not to. He smiled, though – he smiled and smiled! And so did Bunny!

'I think you like each other,' said Katy, because that was her name, of course! 'Yes, I'm sure you do. I hope so, anyway, because you've just got to be friends.' And she gave both of them a happy hug.

'You see, you will sit together on my bed each day,

and cuddle down with me at night,' she explained, tucking Bunny in beside Sailor.

Katy kissed them both goodnight. Then she lay down, closed her eyes, and was soon fast asleep. And then – what a whispering there was beside her!

'You!' said Sailor, in delight. 'What a bit of luck!'

'You!' said Bunny. 'Oh, I can't believe it! What's Katy like?'

'Fine,' said Sailor. 'You'll love her. Oh, Bunny – what lovely times we're going to have! You'll like the other toys here, too, all except a rude monkey – but I won't let him tease you! Fancy, we shall be able to be friends all our lives now!'

That was three years ago – and they are still with Katy, though they don't sleep with her at night now, because she thinks she's too big for that.

'It is nice to have a friend,' Bunny keeps saying. Well, it is, isn't it?

The Best Christmas Tree of All

The Best Christmas
Tree of All

ONE DAY a little red squirrel went hunting for seeds in fir cones. He found plenty and he ate them all. 'I'll have just one more feast,' he said, 'and then I'll have had enough.'

He found one more fir cone with seeds in it – but before he could eat them somebody fired a gun. BANG! The gun was fired by a farmer at a flock of rooks, but the little squirrel didn't know that.

'Someone's shooting at me!' he chattered, and away he went. He dropped down from the big spruce tree he was in, and ran through the wood, and scampered into a garden. He bounded across the front lawn, leapt up on a wall, and into a tree. He disappeared into a big hole there, his little heart beating loudly.

But on the way across the lawn he had dropped his fir cone, and a little dry winged seed fell out of it. It went down a wormhole and was lost.

When the earth was warm and moist the little seed grew. It put out roots and shoots, and soon a very tiny fir tree peeped above the grass.

The house was owned by a cross old lady. She didn't like dogs, she didn't like cats, she didn't like birds, she didn't like children. She only liked herself – goodness knows why! She didn't notice the tiny tree growing in the middle of the front lawn. She didn't even notice that the gardener carefully mowed all round it, but left the tiny tree to grow.

Well, it grew into a dear little Christmas tree, a small spruce fir just like the ones we have in the house at Christmas time. It grew one foot high – two feet high, three feet, four feet! It really was a very nice little tree.

And then one December the cross old lady noticed it. 'What's that tree doing, growing right in the middle of my front lawn?' she said. 'Soon it will be so tall that it will spoil my view of the road. Cut it down!'

But the gardener liked the little tree. He didn't want to cut it down. He went to see the old lady. 'Instead of cutting it down, may I take it up by the roots and set it in a pot and make it into a Christmas tree for children?' he asked.

'Certainly not. I won't have you digging up my trees and selling them to children!' said the old lady. The gardener hadn't meant to sell the tree, of course, but she wouldn't believe him.

'Very well, Madam,' said the gardener. 'I will cut it down after Christmas. I shan't have time before. It's a pity you won't let it be a Christmas tree – it's a perfect shape to dress up with candles and presents!'

'Nonsense!' said the old lady. 'Cut it down!'

But on the day before Christmas her cook had an idea. She slipped out and bought coloured candles and ornaments, and some pretty little toys. After tea, when it was dark, she dressed up the little tree with all the toys and shining ornaments. She hung it with sparkling tinfoil and frost, and she set candles on the branches from top to bottom. She put a small fairy doll on the top – and then she lighted all the candles! There was no wind, so they burned beautifully.

And there stood that little tree in the garden, an enchanted, magical little tree, bright with candles, shining in the darkness! Soon the children saw it, and one by one they came to lean over the fence and watch.

And then the old lady saw it. She stood at her window and stared. What was this lovely thing shining in her garden? It took her right back to her own childhood. She remembered the big trees she had seen decorated – she remembered the toys on them. Why, long, long ago she had danced round a Christmas tree and laughed for joy!

Then she heard the children outside laughing for joy too. She saw their faces in the candlelight. She saw their pointing fingers showing one another the toys on the tree!

'What's this?' she said. 'How has that tree blossomed into something so lovely? Who did it?'

She put on a big coat and went out to see it. The children called to her at once.

'Thank you, Miss Hannah! It's a lovely idea! It's like a magic tree, really truly growing. Thank you for such a lovely treat.'

And then Miss Hannah was ashamed. *She* hadn't thought of this lovely idea! It was her gardener – her cook – somebody else, not herself! Why hadn't *she* thought of it? Was she so old and cross that she couldn't even use a Christmas tree growing in her own garden to give pleasure to the children passing by?

She sent her cook to buy more presents for the tree. She bought more candles. She lighted them herself. She gave the presents away to the children when the candles burnt out. She had a perfectly lovely time, and so did the boys and girls.

And after Christmas, when the gardener came to cut down the tree, she called out to him quite fiercely:

'No, no – don't touch that tree! It's never to be cut down. It's the children's. We'll dress it up every single Christmas.'

Well, she does – and the children all come to see it. 'It's the best Christmas tree of all!' they say. 'The very, very best!' I think it is too. I do wish *you* could see it.

Wanted – A Royal Snow-Digger

Wanted – A Royal Snow-Digger

ONCE UPON a time the Fairy Queen wanted a Royal Snow-digger, who would dig away the snow from her palace gates after a snowstorm. So she sent out Domino the brownie and told him to find somebody. Off he went, the feather in his cap waving merrily. He was sure that anyone would be pleased to be made Royal Snow-digger to Her Majesty the Queen.

First he went to Slicker the grass snake, who lay basking in the sunshine of the pretty autumn day.

'Slicker,' he said, 'will you be Royal Snow-digger to the Queen, and dig away the snow from the palace gates after a snowstorm?'

'What is snow?' asked Slicker in wonder. 'I have never seen it. I sleep all the winter through, Domino, in the hollow tree over there, curled up with my brothers and sisters. I cannot be Royal Snow-digger.'

Domino ran off, disappointed. He went to the cornfield where Dozy the little dormouse used to live – but Dozy had run from the field when the corn was cut and was now in the hazel copse, hunting for fallen nuts. Domino found him there, as fat as butter.

'Dozy,' he said, 'will you be Royal Snow-digger to the Queen and dig away the snow from the palace gates after a snowstorm?'

'Not I!' said Dozy, rubbing his fat little sides. 'I shall sleep all the winter through. See how fat I am! I shall not need any food all the cold-weather time. It is stupid to wake up when it is cold. Far better to sleep. I shall be hidden in a warm bank down in a cosy hole, Domino, when the snow comes. I don't want to dig snow for the queen.'

Domino ran off, quite cross with the fat little

dormouse. He came to where the swallows flew high in the air, and called to them, for he knew that the Fairy Queen was fond of the steel-blue birds.

'Swallows,' he called, 'will you be Royal Snow-digger to the queen and dig away the snow from the palace gates after a snowstorm?'

'Twitter, twitter, Domino!' called the swallows, laughing. 'Why, we shall not be here much longer! We never wait for snow and frost. It is too cold for us in the wintertime here, and besides there are no flies to eat. No, no, we are going to fly away south, far away to the warm countries where nobody has ever seen such a strange thing as snow.'

Domino sighed. He would never find a snow-digger for the queen. It was strange. He wondered who to ask next.

I'll ask the big badger, he thought. *He would make a fine snow-digger, for he has great paws – strong and sturdy.*

So he went to where the badger was walking on the hillside and called to him.

'Hey, Brock the badger!' he cried. 'Will you be Royal Snow-digger to the queen and dig away the snow from the palace gates after a snowstorm?'

'I should like to very much,' said Brock. 'But, you know, Domino, I cannot keep awake in the wintertime. I simply have to go to sleep. I am lining a nice big hole in the hillside now, with all sorts of warm things – dead leaves and bracken and big cushions of moss – to make me and my family a warm bed for the winter. We always sleep through the cold weather.'

'Dear, dear, what lazy creatures you must be!' said Domino, crossly. 'Well, I'll go and find someone else. They can't all be as lazy as you, Brock!'

Soon Domino met the hedgehog, Spiny, and he waved his hand to him brightly.

'Hey, Spiny!' he called. 'Wait a minute! I want to ask you something. Will you be Royal Snow-digger to the queen and dig away the snow from the palace gates after a snowstorm?'

'I'd like to, Domino,' said Spiny, shuffling in the dead leaves. 'But you know, I hide away in the ditch all winter through. I can't bear the cold weather. You won't find me after a snowstorm! No, I cannot be Royal Snow-digger. But look – there goes Crawler the toad. Ask him.'

The toad was crawling on the damp side of the ditch, so Domino jumped across and spoke to him.

'Crawler, will you be Royal Snow-digger to the queen and dig away the snow from the palace gates after a snowstorm?' he asked.

'No,' said Crawler, blinking his lovely coppery eyes, 'I won't. I am a sensible person and I like to sleep under a damp stone when frost and snow are about. It's no use asking my cousins the frogs, either – they sleep upside-down in the pond, tucked comfortably away in the mud at the bottom. Goodbye!'

'There aren't many more people to ask,' said Domino to himself. 'Dear, dear me – I can't possibly go home to the queen and tell her that I can find nobody. She would make *me* Royal Snow-digger and that's a job I should hate! Too much hard work about it for me! Hello, there goes Bushy the squirrel. He's a lively chap. He'd make a splendid snow-digger.'

So he called to Bushy the squirrel, who was hiding nuts away in a hollow tree.

'Bushy! Bushy! Will you be Royal Snow-digger and sweep away the snow from the palace gate after a snowstorm?' he called. 'You don't sleep all the winter, do you?'

'Well, not exactly,' said the squirrel. 'But I only wake up on nice sunny days, Domino. I sleep curled up in my tail in a hollow tree when it's really cold. I'm not sure I would wake up after a snowstorm. In fact, I'm quite sure I couldn't. But you can try to wake me if you like.'

'Oh no, thanks,' said Domino, in disgust. 'I must have someone I can trust to be on the spot. I don't want to go hunting in all the hollow trees in the wood to find you on a snowy day!'

He turned away and went back towards the palace. As he went he heard a little voice calling him. He looked round. It was Bobtail the sandy rabbit.

'I heard what you were asking Bushy the squirrel,' said Bobtail. 'Do you think I would do for Royal Snow-digger, Domino? I'd love to try.'

'Oh, I expect you sleep all the winter, don't you, like the others?' said Domino, gloomily. 'Or you stand on your head in the pond? Or line a hole in a bank and snore there? I don't believe there's any use in asking you to be Royal Snow-digger.'

'Oh, Domino, I keep awake all the winter!' said Bobtail. 'Yes, I do, really. I'm used to the snow. And there is my cousin the hare, too – he's out all the winter. And so are the weasels and the stoats – but don't let's talk of them! They are cruel fellows, and no gentlemen!'

'Well, you can be Royal Snow-digger then,' said Domino. 'Come along to the queen and she will give you your snow-digger badge. But mind, Bobtail, if you suddenly make up your mind to do what nearly all the others do – sleep, or fly away, or hide somewhere – I'll hunt you out and pull your tail.'

'I shan't do any of those things,' said Bobtail, happily. He walked to the palace with Domino the brownie, and the queen hung a little golden badge round his neck. On it was printed ROYAL SNOW-DIGGER.

And now every winter the rabbits are the queen's snow-diggers. They sweep away the snow from the palace gates after a snowstorm, and never dream of going to sleep like the toads and hedgehogs, the badgers and the squirrels.

If you see a rabbit out in the snow, look at him carefully. If he has a golden badge hung round his neck, you'll know what he is – a Royal Snow-digger!

The Pantomime Cat

The Pantomime Cat

'MOLLIE! JOHN!' called Mummy. 'Where are you? I want you a minute.'

The two children were playing out in the garden. They ran in.

'I hear that old Mrs Jones isn't well,' said Mummy. 'She can't go out and do her shopping. Now I think it would be very nice if you two children did her errands for her each day till she is better.'

'Oh, Mummy, I don't like Mrs Jones!' said Mollie. 'She always looks so cross!'

'And she never gives anyone a penny, or a biscuit, or a sweet, or anything,' said John.

'You don't do kind things for the sake of pennies or sweets,' said Mummy. 'You know that. You do it because it is good to be kind. You like me to be kind to you, don't you?'

'Yes,' said Mollie. 'We love you for it, Mummy! All right. We'll go – won't we, John!'

They were good-hearted children, so each day at ten o'clock in the morning they ran up the hill to Mrs Jones's little cottage, knocked at the door and asked her what errands she wanted running.

Mrs Jones never seemed very pleased to see them, and certainly she never gave them anything – not even a sweet out of her peppermint tin. She was not a very kind old lady and although the children were polite to her, and always ran her errands cheerfully, they thought she was a cross old thing, and were glad when they had finished going to the grocer's, the baker's and the fishmonger's each day.

It was the Christmas holidays, and circuses and pantomimes were in every big town. There was a pantomime in the town where Mollie and John lived too, and children often stopped outside the big theatre and looked at the pictures.

'It's *Dick Whittington and His Cat*,' said Mollie. 'Last year it was *Aladdin and the Lamp*. I do wish Mummy would take us, John.'

But Mummy said no, she hadn't enough money for all of them. Perhaps they would go the next year.

'You said that last year, Mummy,' sighed Mollie. 'I do wish we were rich! I'd love to go every night and see Dick Whittington and his clever cat. A girl I know has been, and she says the cat is ever so big and so funny that she laughed till she couldn't laugh any more!'

'Now it's ten o'clock,' said Mummy. 'Off you go to Mrs Jones. You won't have to do her errands much longer because she can walk quite well now. You have been good children to run them so cheerfully.'

Off went Mollie and John up the hill. They knocked at Mrs Jones's door and went in. She was sitting at the table, sewing something with a big needle.

The children looked at it. It was a strange thing she was sewing – like a big, black fur rug – with a cat's head.

'Whatever is that?' asked Mollie, in surprise.

'Always asking questions!' grumbled the disagreeable old woman. 'It's the cat skin my son wears in the pantomime. Didn't you know he was the Cat in *Dick Whittington* this year?'

'Oh, no!' cried both children in delight. 'How perfectly lovely!'

'Hmmm!' said Mrs Jones, snapping off her thread. 'Not so very lovely, I should think – nasty hot thing to wear every night for hours on end. Hmmm! Now listen – my son wants this cat costume this morning before eleven, so pop down now straight away and go to the stage door at the back of the theatre. Ask for Mr Jones and say you've brought his costume. That's all I want you to do today. After this morning I can do all my own shopping, so I won't be seeing you any more.'

She wrapped up the parcel and the children sped off. 'Mean old thing!' said Mollie. 'Never even said thank you to us! I say! What fun to be going in at the stage door of the theatre! We might see some fairies – you know – the ones that sing and dance in the pantomime!'

They soon arrived at the stage door and asked the old man there for Mr Jones.

'Go up the stairs and knock on the second door on the right,' said the old chap. Mollie and John ran up the stone steps and knocked on the second door.

'Come in!' shouted someone – and in they went.

A round, jolly-faced man was sitting in front of a mirror. He smiled when he saw them. 'Hallo!' he said. 'Have you brought my cat skin? Thanks awfully! I say, are you the two children who have been running errands for my mother all this time?'

'Yes,' said Mollie shyly.

'And I guess she never said thank you, did she? Or gave you a penny between you,' laughed the man. 'She's a funny old thing, but she means well. Have you seen me in the pantomime, dressed up in this cat skin?'

'No, we haven't,' said John. 'Mummy can't afford to take us this year – but oh, you must look lovely! I wish we could see you!'

'Well, you shall!' said the jolly man, unwrapping the parcel. 'You shall have free tickets every night of the week, bless your kind little hearts! That's your reward for being kind to someone who never said a word of thanks! I've some free tickets to give away – and my mother never wants to use them – so you shall have them! Would you like that?'

'Oh, yes!' shouted both the children, their faces red with delight. 'Yes, yes, yes! We shall see Dick Whittington – and the fairies – and you – and everything else! Oh, what luck!'

Well, it all came true – they did see the pantomime, every night of the week! The jolly man gave them their tickets, and oh, how they loved every minute of it!

'The cat is the best and funniest of all!' said Mollie and John. 'We do love him! And we are proud of knowing him, Mummy! Fancy knowing the pantomime cat! All the other boys and girls wish they were us!'

'Ah! You didn't know you were running errands for the pantomime cat's mother, did you!' said Mummy. 'You never know what will happen when you do a kindness!'

The Three
Strange Travellers

The Three
Strange Travellers

ONCE UPON a time there was a billy goat who drew a little goat carriage on the sea-sands. He took children for quite a long ride along the beach.

But one day, when he was quite old, he became lame. He limped with his right front foot, and no longer could he draw the goat carriage along at a fine pace.

'You are no use to me now,' said his master, a cross and selfish old man. 'I shall buy a new goat.'

The old billy goat bleated sadly. What would he do if his master no longer needed him?

'You can go loose on the common,' said the old man.

'Don't come to me for a home, for I don't want you any longer.'

Poor billy goat! He was very unhappy. He looked at his little goat carriage for the last time and then he limped off to the common. The winter was coming on and he hoped he would not freeze to death. He had always lived in a cosy shed in the wintertime – but now he would have no home.

He hadn't gone very far across the common when he heard a loud quacking behind him. 'Quack quack! Stop, I say! Hey, stop a minute! Quack!'

The billy goat turned round. He saw a duck waddling along as fast as it could, quacking loudly.

'What's the matter?' he asked.

'Plenty!' said the duck, quite out of breath. 'Do you mind if I walk with you? There are people after me who will kill me if they find me.'

'Mercy on us!' said the goat, startled. 'Why do they want to kill you?'

'Well,' said the duck indignantly, 'I have stopped

laying eggs and my master says I'm no use now, so he wants to eat me for his dinner. And I have served him well for many, many months, laying him delicious eggs, far nicer than any hen's!'

'Dear me,' said the billy goat, 'you and I seem to have the same kind of masters. Maybe they are brothers. Well, Duck, walk with me. I am seeking my fortune, and would be glad of company.'

The two walked on together, the goat limping and the duck waddling. When they reached the end of the common they came to a farm.

'Do not go too near,' said the duck. 'I don't wish to be caught. Do you?'

'No,' said the goat. 'Listen! What's that?'

They stood still and heard a great barking. Suddenly a little dog squeezed itself under a nearby gate and came running towards them. The duck got behind the goat in fright, and the goat stood with his horns lowered in case the dog should attack him.

'Don't be afraid of me,' panted the dog. 'I am

running away. My master has beaten me because I let a fox get two chickens last night. But what could I do? I was chained up and I could not get at the fox. I barked loudly, but my master was too fast asleep to hear me. And now he blames me for the fox's theft!'

'You are to be pitied,' said the goat. 'We, too, have had bad masters. Come with us, and we will keep together and look after ourselves. Maybe we shall find better masters some day.'

'I will come,' said the dog. 'I am getting old, you know, and I cannot see as well as I used to do. I think my master wants to get rid of me and have a younger dog. Ah me, there is no kindness in the world these days!'

The three animals journeyed on together. They ate what they could find. The billy goat munched the green grass; the duck swam on each pond she came to and hunted about in the mud at the bottom for food; the dog sometimes found a bit of bread or a hunk of meat thrown away by the wayside, which he gobbled greedily.

They walked for miles and miles. Often the goat and the dog gave the duck a ride on their backs for she waddled so slowly and soon got tired. At night they found a sheltered place beneath a bush, or beside a haystack, and slept there in a heap, the duck safely in the middle.

They became very fond of one another and vowed they would never separate. But as the days grew colder the three creatures became anxious.

'When the ponds are frozen I shall find no food,' said the duck.

'And I shall not be able to eat grass when everywhere is covered with snow,' said the goat. 'I shall freeze to death at night, too, for I have always been used to a shed in the winter.'

'And I have been used to a warm kennel,' said the dog. 'What shall we do?' They could think of no plan, so on they wandered.

Then one afternoon a great snowstorm blew up. The blizzard was so strong that even the soft snowflakes stung their eyes.

'We shall be completely lost in this dreadful storm!' barked the dog. 'We must find shelter.'

The goat and the duck followed him. He put his nose to the ground and ran off. He went up a little hill and at last came to a small cottage. There was a light in one of the windows.

'Somebody lives here,' said the dog. 'Let us knock at the door and ask for shelter.'

So the goat tapped the door with his hoof. He bleated as he did so, and the dog whined and the duck quacked.

Inside the cottage was an old woman with a red shawl round her shoulders. She was darning a hole in a stocking, and thinking about the dreadful storm. Suddenly she heard the tap-tap-tapping at her door.

'Bless us!' she cried, in a fright. 'There's someone

there! Shall I open the door or not? It may be a robber come through the storm to rob me of the gold pieces I have hidden so carefully in my old stocking under the mattress! No, I dare not open the door!'

As she sat trembling she heard the dog whining. Then she heard the bleating of the goat and the anxious quacking of the duck.

'Well, well!' she said in astonishment. 'It sounds for all the world like a dog, a goat and a duck! But how do they come to my door like this? Do they need shelter from this terrible storm, poor things? Well, I have no shed to put them in, so they must come in here with me.'

She got up and went to the door. She undid the bolt and opened the door a crack. When she saw the trembling goat, the shivering dog and the frightened duck her kind heart melted at once and she opened the door wide.

'Poor lost creatures!' she said. 'Come in, come in. You shall have warmth and shelter while this storm lasts. Then I've no doubt you will want to go back to your homes.'

The three animals came gladly in to the warmth. The dog at once lay down on the hearth rug, the goat stood near by, and the duck lay down in a corner, put her head under her wing and fell fast asleep, for she was very tired.

The old woman didn't know what to make of the three creatures. They seemed to know one another so well, and by the way they bleated, barked and quacked to one another they could talk as well as she could.

The goat was very thin, and the dog was skinny, too. As for the duck, when the old woman felt her, she was nothing but feathers and bone!

'The poor creatures,' said the kind old dame. 'They are starving. Well, I will give them a good meal to eat – they will feel all the better for it.'

So she began to cook a meal of all the household scraps she had – bits of meat, vegetables, potatoes, bread, all sorts. How good it smelt! Even the duck in the corner stuck out her head from under her wing to have a sniff.

The old woman took the big saucepan off the fire and stood it on the windowsill to cool. Then she ladled the warm food out into three dishes and put one in front of each animal.

'There, my dears,' she said, 'eat that and be happy tonight.'

Well, the three animals could hardly believe their eyes to see such kindness! They gobbled up the food and left not a single scrap. Then the goat rubbed his head gently against the old dame's knee, the dog licked her hand and the duck laid her head on her shoe. Then they all curled up in a heap together and fell asleep. The old dame went to her bed and slept, too.

In the morning the storm was over. The countryside was covered with snow. The animals did not want to leave the warm cottage, but the old woman opened the door.

'Now you must find your way home,' she said. She

did not know that they had no homes. She thought they had got lost in the storm, and that now they would be glad to go out and find their way back to their homes.

The animals were sad. They took leave of the kind woman, and wished they could tell her that they would like to stay. But she could not understand their language. They went out into the snow, and wondered where to go next.

'Let us go down the hill,' said the goat. 'See, there are some haystacks there and we may be able to find some food and shelter under the stacks tonight.'

So down the hill they went. But they could not find any food. They crouched under the haystack that evening and tried to get warm. As they lay there, quite still, they heard the sound of soft footsteps in the snow. Then they heard voices.

'The old woman has a great hoard of gold,' said one voice. 'We will go to her cottage tonight, when she is in bed, and steal it.'

'Very well,' said the second voice. 'I will meet you there, and we will share the gold. She has no dog to bark or bite.'

The animals listened in horror. Why, it must be the kind old woman these horrid men were speaking of! How could they save her from the robbers?

'We must go back to the cottage,' said the dog. 'Somehow we must creep in and wait for these robbers. Then we will set on them and give them the fright of their lives!'

So the three limped, walked and waddled all the way up the hill again until they came to the little cottage. The old woman was just going to bed. The goat peeped in at the window and saw her blow her candle out.

'She has left this window a little bit open,' he said to the dog. 'Can you jump in and open the door for me and the duck?'

'Yes,' said the dog, 'I can do that. I often saw my master open the farm doors. I know how to.'

He squeezed in through the window and went to the door. He pulled at the latch and the door opened. It was not bolted, so the goat and the duck came in at once. They could hear the old dame snoring.

'What shall we do when the robbers come?' asked the duck excitedly.

'I have a plan,' said the goat. 'You, duck, shall first of all frighten the robbers by quacking at the top of your very loud voice. You, dog, shall fly at the legs of the first robber, and I will lower my head and butt the second one right in the middle. Ha, what a fright we will give them!'

The three animals were so excited that they could hardly keep still. The duck flew up on the table and stood there. The dog hid behind the door. The goat stood ready on the hearth rug, for he wanted a good run when he butted the second robber.

Presently the dog's sharp ears told him that the two robbers were outside. He warned the others and they got ready to do their parts. The robbers pushed the door open.

At that moment the duck opened her beak and quacked as loudly as she could. How she quacked! Quack! Quack! Quack! Quack! Quack!

Then the dog flew at the legs of the first robber and bit them. And he growled. Grrrr! Grrrr! Wuff! Wuff! Wuff! What a terrible noise it was!

Then the goat ran at the second robber and butted him so hard in the middle that he sat down suddenly and lost all his breath.

The duck was so excited that she wanted to join in the fun. So she flew at the robbers and pecked their noses hard. Peck! Peck!

The robbers were frightened almost out of their lives. They couldn't think what was happening! There was such a terrible noise going on, and something was biting, hitting and pecking them from top to toe. How they wished they had never come near the cottage!

As soon as they could, they got to their feet and ran. The duck flew after them and pecked their ankles. The dog tore pieces out of their trousers. The goat limped as fast as he could and butted them down the hill. My, what a set-to it was!

The two robbers fell into a ditch and covered themselves with mud.

'That old woman is a witch!' cried one.

'Yes, she pinched my ears!' said the other. 'And she bit my legs!'

'Ho, and she punched me in the middle so that I lost all my breath!' said the first.

'And all the time she was making such a noise!' cried the second, trying to clamber out of the ditch. 'She said, "Whack! Whack! Whack!"'

'Yes, and she cried, "Cuff! Cuff! Cuff!" too!' said the first. 'And how she chased us down the hill!'

The three animals laughed till the tears came into their eyes when they heard the robbers talking like this.

'They thought my "Quack! Quack! Quack!" was "Whack! Whack! Whack!"' said the duck, in delight.

'And they thought my "Wuff! Wuff! Wuff!" was "Cuff! Cuff! Cuff!"' said the dog, jumping about joyfully. 'What a joke! How we frightened them!'

'Let us go back and see if the old dame is all right,' said the goat. 'She awoke when the duck began to quack.'

Back they all went to the cottage, and found the old dame sitting up in bed, trembling, with a lighted candle by her side. When she saw the three animals she could hardly believe her eyes.

'So it was you who set upon those robbers and chased them away!' she said. 'You dear, kind, clever creatures! Why, I thought you had gone to your homes!'

The goat went up to the bed and put his front paws there. The dog put his nose on the quilt. The duck flew up on the bedrail and flapped her wings.

'Wuff!' said the dog, meaning, 'We want to stay with you!'

'Bleat!' said the goat, and meant the same thing.

'Quack!' said the duck, and she meant the same thing, too.

And this time the old dame understood them, and she smiled joyfully.

'So you want to stay here?' she said. 'Well, you shall. I'm all alone and I want company. It's wintertime and I expect you need shelter, so you shall all live with me. I shall always be grateful to you for chasing away those robbers.'

Well, those three animals soon settled down with the old woman. The duck laid her an egg for her breakfast each day. The dog lay on the doormat and guarded the cottage for her each night. The goat was troubled because he could do nothing for his kind mistress.

But one day he found how well he could help her. She had to go to the woods to get firewood. She took with her a little cart to bring it back, and this she had to pull herself, for she had no pony.

But the goat stood himself in the shafts and bleated.

The old woman saw that he wanted her to tie the cart to him so that he might pull the wood home for her, and she was delighted. Every day after that the goat took the cart to the woods for his mistress and very happy they were together.

As for the robbers, they have never dared to come back. They went a hundred miles away, and told the people there a marvellous story of an old witch who cried 'Whack! Cuff! Whack! Cuff!' and could bite, pinch and punch all at once. But nobody believed them.

The old dame and the dog, goat and duck still live together very happily. Their house is called Windy Cottage, so if ever you pass by, go in and see them all. The old dame will love to tell you the story of how they came to live together!

Mr Twiddle
and the Snow

Mr Twiddle
and the Snow

IT WAS a very snowy day. Mr Twiddle hoped that Mrs Twiddle wouldn't want him to go out in it. It was difficult to walk in thick snow, and Mr Twiddle felt he would much rather sit by the fire and read the paper.

But soon he heard Mrs Twiddle's voice. 'I hope you are not going to sit indoors this fine day, Twiddle. The sun is out now. It will do you good to go out. Will you fetch me some fish from the fishmonger's?'

Twiddle groaned. He knew he would have to. He put on his galoshes and his coat and hat, took a basket and set out. The children were having a fine time that day. They were making snowballs and throwing them, they were building snowmen, and they were sliding down the big hill nearby on sledges.

Mr Twiddle had quite a time dodging snowballs and sledges. Then he stood still and watched some children at the top of the hill, making a very big snowball indeed.

'We're going to roll it down the hill and it will get bigger and bigger,' they cried. Mr Twiddle watched as they began to roll the big ball downwards.

Halfway down it was very big indeed. Then it began to roll down by itself, like a round avalanche. It came down more and more quickly, and Twiddle tried to hop out of the way. But he was just too late and the great big snowball struck him very hard indeed.

Mr Twiddle was knocked right over. Then he was taken onwards with the snowball, which was still rolling and gathering more snow. On and on he went, rolling over and over, getting the snow all round him. Then the snowball stopped, in the middle of the village street, which just then happened to be empty.

'Didn't it roll well!' shouted the children on the hill. 'Let's make another.'

They hadn't seen that their snowball had knocked down and taken Mr Twiddle along with it. They set to work to make another.

Mr Twiddle was buried in the middle of the big snowball. He didn't like it. He had snow down his neck, and in his mouth, ears and nose. It was cold and horrid. Mr Twiddle began to struggle and groan.

An old lady came by and she looked in alarm at the snowball. What peculiar noises were coming out of it! What was the matter with it?

Grrrrrr, said Twiddle, growling with anger in the middle of the snowball, trying to get his head out. A little dog came up and barked in excitement.

The old lady hurried off to tell a policeman. 'There's a snowball behaving in a very strange manner,' she told him. 'Right in the middle of the village street. It said *Grrrrrr* just like a dog.'

'I'll look into the matter,' said the policeman, looking surprised. He went off to the snowball and looked at it. What a big one! And what noises came from it! He scratched his head and wondered if he ought to arrest a snowball.

Presently some more people came up and looked at the snowball, which was now wriggling a bit here and there, and was still making strange noises.

'What is it?' said everyone. 'Is there some animal inside? Who put the snowball here?'

Suddenly out shot Mr Twiddle's head, and he blinked round at everyone in surprise. The policeman jumped and stared. Why, this must be some sort of a snowman! He took out his notebook.

'How did you get into the snow? Are you pretending to be a snowman? Did you build the snow up all round yourself?' cried the people, in surprise.

'Help me out,' said Mr Twiddle. 'I've lost my glasses in the snow.'

'I'll have to arrest you for obstructing the traffic,'

said the policeman, and wrote in his notebook.

'How can I obstruct traffic when there isn't any?' said Twiddle, indignantly, trying to get his arms out of the snowball.

'Well, you would have obstructed it if there had been any,' said the policeman. 'You come along with me.'

'How can I? I'm in the middle of this big snowball,' said Twiddle. 'Do you suppose I like being here? Nobody helps me at all!'

'Well, you got yourself in, so I suppose you can get yourself out,' said the policeman.

'When I get out I'm going to tell you a few things,' said Twiddle, angrily, 'and I shouldn't be a bit surprised to find myself pulling your nose!'

'Now, now, look here, you can't talk to the police like that!' said the policeman, crossly. 'As soon as you're out of that snowball I'm going to take you straight to the police station!'

That made Twiddle feel upset. He didn't want to

be marched off to the police station. What would Mrs Twiddle say if she heard he was locked up? He would never hear the last of it.

He stopped trying to get out of the big snowball. Perhaps if he stayed there quietly the policeman would get tired of waiting and would go away. But he didn't. He began to scrape at the snow to free Twiddle. He badly wanted to take him off to the police station now. He would show Twiddle that he couldn't talk about pulling noses!

Goodness knows what would have happened if the children at the top of the hill hadn't sent down another enormous snowball! It came bounding down the hill, getting bigger and bigger as it came. It shot into the village street, and arrived at top speed just where the crowd stood, watching Twiddle.

In a second everyone was bowled over, and buried in the snow, for the snowball burst all over them. The policeman was right underneath. He lost his helmet, his notebook and his temper.

As soon as Twiddle saw everyone on the ground, groping about wildly, he saw his chance of escape. He struck out at the snow surrounding him, managed to get free, found his glasses, and rushed off home. He didn't stop till he got there. Then he put on his glasses, brushed down his coat, and went indoors.

Well, he thought, as he sat down in his chair and picked up the paper. *Well – I'm not going out again today for anyone in the world! What a time I've had! Nearly buried in snow – almost taken off to prison – well, well, well.*

'Is that you, Twiddle?' called Mrs Twiddle. 'Put the fish in the larder, will you?'

Twiddle frowned and rubbed his nose. He had forgotten all about the fish! Now what was he to do? Well, he wouldn't say anything at all, and perhaps Mrs Twiddle wouldn't notice the fish wasn't there, till the next day when she wanted to cook it.

But she did notice it. She went to the larder to cut a bit off the fish for the cat – and to her surprise there was no fish there!

'Twiddle! There's no fish! The cat must have had it! How many times have I told you not to leave the larder door open?'

'About six-hundred times,' said Twiddle, politely.

'Don't be rude,' said Mrs Twiddle. 'Well, what a waste – to think all that fish is inside the cat. Go and put on your hat and coat and fetch some more.'

Twiddle groaned. He went to fetch his hat and coat and then Mrs Twiddle appeared too, dressed ready to go out. 'It's such a nice afternoon,' she said. 'I thought I would come with you.'

'Well, if you're going out, I may as well stay at home,' said Twiddle, pleased, and took off his hat. But no, he had to go, to keep Mrs Twiddle company.

On the way they met the policeman, who had a black eye because someone had kicked him by accident when they had all been knocked over by the snowball. Mrs Twiddle was very sorry to see it.

'Ah,' said the policeman, stroking his eye gently.

'Ah, I had a bad time this morning. I was just about to make an arrest of a man who was obstructing the traffic and being very rude to me, when a big snowball knocked me down, and my prisoner escaped.'

'What bad luck!' said Mrs Twiddle. 'Fancy the man being rude to you! I wonder that he dared to.'

'He said he would pull my nose,' said the policeman. Mrs Twiddle clicked her tongue in horror, and then walked on with Twiddle, who hadn't said a word all the time.

'Would you believe it!' said Mrs Twiddle, in a tone of horror. 'Well, Twiddle, silly though you are sometimes, I'm quite sure you would never be rude to a policeman.'

And still Twiddle never said a word. Well, there wasn't anything he could say! Poor Twiddle.

Acknowledgements

All efforts have been made to seek necessary permissions.

The stories in this publication first appeared in the following publications:

'Santa's Workshop' first appeared as 'Whiskers for the Cat' in *Sunny Stories*, No. 366, 1945.

'Christmas at Last!' first appeared as Chapter 18 and Chapter 19 in *Bimbo and Topsy*, 1943.

'The Christmas Pudding that Wouldn't Stop' first appeared in *Sunny Stories for Little Folks*, No. 11, 1926.

'The Wishing Glove' first appeared in *Sunny Stories for Little Folks*, No. 11, 1926.

'Mr Icy-Cold' first appeared as 'Mister Icy-Cold' in *Sunny Stories*, No. 52, 1938.

'The Fairies' Christmas Party' first appeared as 'Peggy's Musical Box' in *Sunny Stories for Little Folks*, No. 141, 1932.

'The Christmas Party' first appeared in *The Teachers World*, No. 1492, 1931.

'Pins and Needles!' first appeared in *Sunday Mail*, No. 1942, 1945.

'Mr Loud-Voice Makes a Mistake' first appeared in *Enid Blyton's Magazine*, No. 26, Vol. 3, 1955.

'What's Happened to Michael?' first appeared in *Sunny Stories*, No. 446, 1948.

'Mr Widdle's Christmas Stocking' first appeared in *The Teachers World*, No. 1752, 1936.

'Who Could It Be?' first appeared in *Enid Blyton's Magazine*, No. 25, Vol. 3, 1955.

'The Battle in the Toyshop' first appeared as 'The Battle in the Toy-Shop' in *Sunny Stories for Little Folks*, No. 157, 1933.

'Surprise on Christmas Morning' first appeared in *Enid Blyton's Magazine*, No. 26, Vol. 3, 1955.

'Rescuing Santa Claus' first appeared in *The Teacher's World*, No. 1250, 1927.

'The Astonishing Christmas Tree' first appeared in *The Teachers World*, No. 1191, 1926.

'A Christmas Story' first appeared in *The Teachers World*, No. 1386, 1929.

'Do-As-You're-Told!' first appeared in *Sunny Stories for Little Folks*, No. 106, 1939.

'Something in His Stocking' first appeared in *Enid Blyton's Magazine*, No. 25, Vol. 2, 1954.

'Mr Pink-Whistle and Santa Claus' first appeared in *Enid Blyton's Magazine*, No. 26, Vol. 5, 1957.

'On Christmas Night' first appeared in *Good Housekeeping*, Dec. 1945.

'The Great Big Snowman' first appeared in *Sunny Stories*, No. 2, 1937.

'Peter's Christmas Surprise' first appeared as 'One Christmas Night' in *The Teachers World*, No. 1543, 1932.

'Bunny's First Christmas' first appeared as 'It's Christmas-Time' in *Enid Blyton's Magazine*, No. 26, Vol. 2, 1954.

'The Best Christmas Tree of All' first appeared in *Enid Blyton's Sunny Stories*, No. 496, 1950.

'Wanted – A Royal Snow-Digger' first appeared in *Sunny Stories for Little Folks*, No. 181, 1934.

'The Pantomime Cat' first appeared in *Sunny Stories for Little Folks*, No. 247, 1936.

'The Three Strange Travellers' first appeared in *Sunny Stories for Little Folks*, No. 165, 1933.

'Mr Twiddle and the Snow' first appeared in *Enid Blyton's Sunny Stories*, No. 347, 1945.

Join the Adventure
THE FAMOUS FIVE

Five on a Treasure Island

Five Run Away Together

Five Go to Smuggler's Top

Five Go Off in a Caravan

Five on Kirrin Island Again

Five Go Off to Camp

Five Get Into Trouble

Five Fall Into Adventure

Have you read them all?

More classic stories from the world of

Enid Blyton

The Famous Five Colour Short Stories

Enid Blyton also wrote eight short stories about the
Famous Five. Here they are, in their original texts,
with brand-new illustrations. They're a perfect
introduction to the gang, and an exciting new way to
enjoy classic Blyton stories.

Do you want to solve a mystery?

Enid Blyton

The Secret Seven

Join Peter, Janet, Jack, Barbara, Pam, Colin, George
and Scamper as they solve puzzles and mysteries,
foil baddies, and rescue people from danger – all without
help from the grown-ups. Enid Blyton wrote fifteen
stories about the Secret Seven. These editions contain
brilliant illustrations by Tony Ross, plus extra
fun facts and stories to read and share.

Enid Blyton

is one of the most popular children's authors of all time. Her books have sold over 500 million copies and have been translated into other languages more often than any other children's author.

Enid Blyton adored writing for children. She wrote over 600 books and hundreds of short stories. *The Famous Five* books, now 75 years old, are her most popular. She is also the author of other favourites including *The Secret Seven*, *The Magic Faraway Tree*, *Malory Towers* and *Noddy*.

Born in London in 1897, Enid lived much of her life in Buckinghamshire and adored dogs, gardening and the countryside. She was very knowledgeable about trees, flowers, birds and animals.

Dorset – where some of the Famous Five's adventures are set – was a favourite place of hers too.

Enid Blyton's stories are read and loved by millions of children (and grown-ups) all over the world. Visit enidblyton.co.uk to discover more.